W9-BGK-368

Dreams of a Highlander

Katy Baker

Published by Katy Baker, 2016.

While every precaution has been taken in the preparation of this book, the publisher assumes no responsibility for errors or omissions, or for damages resulting from the use of the information contained herein.

DREAMS OF A HIGHLANDER

First edition. August 30, 2016.

Copyright © 2016 Katy Baker.

Written by Katy Baker.

Chapter 1

"Careful, Doctor, he bites," said Mrs Wright.

The warning came too late. Fluffy, her huge Persian cat, yowled and sunk his teeth into Darcy's hand. Darcy bit her lip, determined not to curse in front of a client. Even though she wore a reinforced glove made for this very purpose, Fluffy had managed to find its weak spot - the stitching around the wrist. He twisted in her grip and swiped with a front paw, claws extended.

"Stop that!" Darcy said in a commanding voice. "If you don't behave, I'll have to sedate you."

This time Fluffy had eaten a ping-pong ball belonging to one of Mrs Wright's grandchildren. Last month it was a dish cloth. The time before that, a pair of shoelaces.

"I can't feel any large masses," Darcy said. "Which suggests he chewed it up pretty thoroughly before he swallowed it. He should be fine but if he shows signs of pain, bring him back."

She released Fluffy who leapt into his owner's arms and fixed Darcy with a hateful stare.

"That's a relief," said Mrs Wright. "Thank you for your time, Doctor. Sorry about your hand."

Darcy smiled, pulling off the gloves. "All part of the service. Glad I could help."

It was late. The clock on the consultation room wall read 8.05pm. Darcy should have finished work three hours ago but the practice had been inundated with emergencies and Darcy stayed to help out.

She escorted Mrs Wright to the door then flopped onto her chair, stretching her hands over her head and yawning.

There was a knock on the door. Gretchen Matthews, Darcy's best friend, stuck her head around it. "Has the devil cat gone? Is it safe to come in?"

Gretchen was bubbly, blonde and easy-going. In many ways she and Darcy were polar opposites but they'd been best friends ever since they'd met at veterinary college.

"It's safe," Darcy laughed, waving for her friend to come in. "Hopefully he might learn his lesson."

Gretchen rolled her eyes at that. "Chance would be a fine thing. That cat has a death-wish. The emergencies have all been dealt with. How about we go for a drink? It's been a hell of a day."

That sounded good. "Sure," Darcy said, rising. "Let's make a run for it before anything else happens."

They knocked off and made their way to the nearest bar - a place Gretchen and the others often visited although Darcy rarely joined them. They got themselves a couple of drinks and slumped onto a leather sofa by the window.

"So," Gretchen said around a mouthful of peanuts. "You sorted it yet?"

Darcy groaned. She should have known this question was coming. She knew exactly what Gretchen was talking about. "Not yet," she replied. "I've been too busy."

Gretchen rolled her eyes. "Too busy? That's always your excuse!"

"It's true," Darcy said. "When do I have time for romance? I'm in early clinic for the rest of the week, I'm doing a guest lecture at the University on Friday- which I haven't even begun to prep for - and I'm off to that conference in Edinburgh next week!"

Gretchen pursed her lips and frowned at Darcy in a way that suggested she didn't buy any of her friend's excuses. Okay, so it was true that Darcy had *volunteered* for all the things she'd just listed. She was dedicated to her job, what was wrong with that?

"Fine," Gretchen said. "Then how about letting me give you a helping hand? Have you even checked your responses yet?"

"Um no," Darcy replied. "I haven't quite got round to it."

"You're hopeless, you know that?" Gretchen grabbed Darcy's cell phone from where it rested on the table.

"What are you doing?"

"What I said. Giving you a helping hand."

Gretchen tapped a few buttons on the cell. She got up the dating website that she'd enrolled Darcy on and was busy logging into her profile. Darcy cringed as a cheesy photo of herself popped up. She thought it made her look goofy but Gretchen assured her that the big wide smile, combined with her olive skin and long dark hair would have men falling over themselves to message her.

"Let's see," Gretchen said. She began scrolling through the messages. "How about this guy? He's cute."

Darcy examined the picture. "No, I don't think so. It says he likes clubbing. Hardly my scene is it?"

Gretchen frowned. "Okay. How about this one then? He's an animal lover and likes cozy nights in."

"And lives upstate," Darcy said. "I don't want to drive miles to meet a guy."

"Darcy, you're gonna have to take some chances," Gretchen said, her tone exasperated. "There's more to life than work. You're too serious. You need to have a little fun!"

Darcy said nothing. Perhaps Gretchen was right. Perhaps that was why Darcy never had any luck with men. She wasn't interested in relationships that rested on superficial things. When she found the right man, she wanted him to be the only one. The one that she would share her life with. So she'd always taken her relationships seriously, but they had never done the same.

She waved a hand at Gretchen. "Sure. Whatever you say. As soon as I get back from the conference, I'll get on it."

With a sigh Gretchen put Darcy's cell back on the table. "Running away again, eh?"

Darcy straightened. "What's that supposed to mean?"

"Oh come, on," Gretchen said. "It's what you always do. Do you remember when we were at college and Jimmy was going to ask you to move in with him? You suddenly had an aunt who took sick and needed nursing."

"That was true! And things hadn't been right between me and Jimmy for ages anyway!"

"And what about when you caught Ryan with that girl from the student bar? You took off for days."

"Can you blame me?" Darcy said. "It was horrible walking in on them like that. It was either get the hell out of there or slap them both! I didn't fancy getting arrested for assault!"

Gretchen held up her hands. "I know, honey. I know. It's just that now you're off to Edinburgh, seems to me you're running again."

Darcy folded her arms. "It's a conference that's been booked for months."

"Okay," Gretchen sighed. "Okay. Just promise me one thing will you? While you're over there how about you take some time off? See a bit of the country? Relax a little."

Darcy opened her mouth for a retort. She hadn't come here to be lectured by her friend, she'd come to relax after a hard day. But one look at the concern shining in Gretchen's eyes made her hesitate. Was Gretchen right? Did she work too hard? Did she always run away when things got tough? Her parents had died just before she started college and since then she'd felt...adrift. Like she didn't belong anywhere. Was that what she was searching for? A place to belong?

Darcy sighed. "Okay, you win. I'll take some time off. I'll have a vacation whilst I'm over in Scotland. I promise to come back all relaxed. Happy?"

"Great," said Gretchen, grinning. "Now, how about another drink?"

Darcy stepped down from the lectern. The cavernous hall echoed with applause. Her legs were wobbly as she walked down the steps and onto the stage but she was also filled with a sense of euphoria. She'd done it! Her guest lecture on equine dentistry had gone better than she'd dared hope.

Before stepping up onto the lectern she'd been so nervous she thought she might throw up. Before her on the schedule had been professors and highly regarded specialists who she'd idolized during her time in college. And here she was, just a couple of years out of veterinary school, rubbing shoulders with them.

She blew out a breath and stepped through the curtain at the back of the stage and leaned against the wall, trying to still her thumping heart and steady her weak knees.

She'd been in Scotland for three days now. She loved Edinburgh. The architecture, the landscape, the people. Even though she was technically here on business, she found herself relaxing.

Gretchen was right, she thought. *I really do need a break.*

The conference finished that afternoon but Darcy hadn't booked her flight home for another week. She was going to take her friend's advice and see a little of the country before she went home.

She pushed herself away from the wall and made her way through to the refreshments area. The plush bar was all but empty as most delegates were still in the main hall waiting for the next speaker.

Darcy hopped up onto a stool by the bar and ordered herself a lemonade. She gazed out of the window as she sipped it.

Edinburgh's skyline met her gaze and beyond rose the imposing edifice of King Arthur's Seat.

"That was a most interesting talk."

Darcy turned to find a woman sitting on the stool next to hers. Darcy hadn't heard her approach. The woman looked to be in her seventies. She wore a sharp business suit with a deer-shaped brooch pinned to a lapel. Her gray hair was gathered in a bun at the back of her head.

"Thanks," said Darcy. "Although equine dentistry isn't the most interesting of topics. I'm surprised any of the delegates are still awake."

"Och!" the woman said, waving a hand. "Ye do yerself a disservice. Ye have an engaging way about ye, Darcy Greenway."

"How did you know my name?"

"Well, ye did introduce yerself at the start of yer talk. And yer name is on the schedule. Bit of a giveaway don't ye think?"

"Oh, of course," Darcy stammered, feeling a little stupid. "And you are?"

"Irene. Irene MacAskill."

"Pleased to meet you." Darcy held her hand out to the woman who shook it. "What brings you to the conference? Do you specialize in any particular area?"

"Me? Och, no. I'm here in another capacity."

"Oh? And what's that?"

A mischievous smile played across Irene MacAskill's face but she didn't answer Darcy's question. "How are ye finding my bonny homeland?"

"It's wonderful," Darcy said. "Although I've not seen much so far. I'm planning on rectifying that though."

Irene cocked her head and regarded Darcy with an unblinking gaze. Darcy found her scrutiny a little uncomfortable.

"Um, are you local to Edinburgh?" Darcy asked.

"Nae, lass."

"Oh. Have you traveled a long way then?"

Irene waved a hand. "Ye could say that. I'm from here and there and nowhere. I come and go as I need to when I'm about my business."

Darcy nodded. She was finding talking to Irene a little strange. She finished her lemonade and placed the empty glass on the bar. "Well, it was nice to meet you. If you'll excuse me-"

Irene's hand shot out and grabbed her wrist. "If ye want to see more of my bonny land, I'll give ye some advice." She placed a small pocket book on the bar. On it was written, *A guide to lochs of the Highlands*. "I've marked in there the path I think ye should take."

Darcy looked at the old woman. Irene stared back, unblinking. "I haven't decided where I'm going yet," she said. "I was going to go to the tourist information office."

"Ye'd do well to take my advice, lass."

Darcy swallowed. "And why's that?"

"Because if ye do, ye might just find yer heart's desire. But ye'll have a difficult choice to make. Nothing good ever comes easy. Remember what I've told ye."

With that Irene released her and hopped down from her stool and left. Darcy watched her go, feeling a little unsettled. The guidebook still sat on the bar. Darcy stood and took a few paces before hesitating. She looked back. Then, on impulse she grabbed the guidebook the old woman had left for her.

She wasn't sure why she did it. The woman hadn't made much sense. And yet...there was something in the way she'd looked at Darcy, as though she could see right into her soul.

Don't be stupid, Darcy said to herself. *She was just an eccentric old woman. She doesn't know you. She doesn't know anything about you.*

Yet as Darcy made her way back into the main hall to listen to the next speaker, she was careful to tuck Irene's guidebook safely into her pocket.

Chapter 2

Quinn MacFarlane crouched on the trail to examine the object that had caught his eye. It was a roasted chicken bone, obviously discarded by the people he was following. The brigands were careless to leave such an obvious clue to their trail.

Careless or overconfident.

Quinn straightened and looked around. The empty wilds of the Highlands surrounded him. In the distance white-capped mountains rose. A village nestled at the base of one of those mountains and Quinn spotted smoke rising from chimneys but it was many miles distant and in the opposite direction to the one his quarry had taken.

The brigands he was tracking had been raiding MacFarlane lands for months now. With each attack they got bolder. Quinn frowned. Their overconfidence would be their downfall. Quinn would find them, he would discover where they were based, and clan MacFarlane would defeat them once and for all.

It was getting late. The sun was starting to sink behind the mountains, sending red streamers of light across the landscape. Quinn hesitated. He ought to return home and report what he'd seen but that meant risking losing the trail. Quinn couldn't do that. He had a duty to his clan, his people.

He took the reins of his large black warhorse, Silver, and led him to a rocky outcrop. The base of the outcrop formed a sheltered dell where he could build a campfire away from prying eyes.

Like any good warrior, Quinn saw to his horse first. He rubbed Silver down then gave him food and water before building a small campfire and laying his blankets by the side. He unbuckled his sword and placed it on the ground close to him where he could grab it quickly if needs be.

He began roasting the grouse he'd caught earlier and sat back, resting against the rocks which were warm from the heat of the day.

Suddenly Silver raised his head and whinnied. A shape moved beyond the edge of the firelight. Quinn was on his feet in an instant, sword held in both hands.

"Who goes there?" he demanded. "Reveal yerself!"

To his surprise, a woman stepped into the light. She was old enough to be Quinn's grandmother and had gray hair caught in a bun at the back of her head. He didn't recognize the colors in the plaid she wore which meant he couldn't name her clan.

She stepped closer and then stopped with hands clasped in front of her, watching him with a sharp gaze. On her shoulder, Quinn noticed, her plaid was held with a brooch shaped like a red deer.

Quinn looked around carefully for her companions but the woman appeared to be alone. "Good evening. How can I help ye?" he asked. "Are ye out here alone?"

The woman nodded. "I am at that, laddie. Seems I wandered far from where I was supposed to be." She cocked her head and a mischievous glint came into her eyes. "Or maybe it's the other way around and I'm exactly where I was supposed to be, eh?"

"If yer on yer way to Glenhowe, yer a fair way from yer path," Quinn said, naming the settlement at the base of the mountains. "Ye'll not make it tonight, that's for sure."

"No, I fear ye may be right," the woman said, smiling.

Quinn frowned. The old woman seemed a little confused. Why was she wandering out here alone at night? It wasn't safe. Didn't she realize that? And where were her kinfolk? They shouldn't let her go wandering.

Quinn sheathed his sword and gestured to the fire. "It isnae much but yer welcome to share my fire and my food."

The old woman broke into a beaming smile. It made her look much younger. "Ah, yer a good one, laddie. I think I chose well in ye."

Quinn wasn't sure what to make of that last statement. He grabbed one of his blankets and laid it out for her on the other side of the fire. She lowered herself gingerly then held her hands out to the flames.

"Och, but that's good. My old bones do ache so these days."

Quinn seated himself and watched the woman from across the fire. "I'm Quinn MacFarlane," he said. "Pleased to make yer acquaintance."

"Oh, I know who ye are, lad."

"Ye do?" Quinn frowned. "I've never met ye before, I'm sure. Who are ye?"

"My name's Irene," the woman replied. "Irene MacAskill."

Quinn froze. He'd heard the name before. Rumors of this woman stalked the Highlands like ghosts. It was said that when she appeared, mischief usually followed.

Irene laughed lightly. "Ah, I can see from ye face that ye recognize my name! Dinna worry lad, I'm not going to turn ye into a toad or suchlike! The tales about me are greatly exaggerated!"

Quinn didn't know what to say to that. He busied himself with taking the grouse from the spit and dividing it into two portions. One portion he passed to Irene. She took it and began stuffing pieces into her mouth greedily.

"My, my, this is good. I do declare ye may be one of the best cooks in the MacFarlane clan!"

Quinn didn't answer. He watched Irene while he ate. "Why are ye out here?" he asked.

She held up a finger. "I might ask the same of ye, laddie. I'm here for the same reason as ye. I'm looking for something. Or I was, anyway. Seems I've found it. Question is, what are ye looking for?"

"Brigands," Quinn answered. "They've been raiding our lands."

She leaned forward. Her eyes gleamed with reflected firelight. "So ye claim. Yet ye could have returned with yer news to the castle. Instead ye chose to stay out here alone. Why is that?"

Quinn didn't like the way she watched him. Her words made him uncomfortable. It was true that he often felt more at peace out here away from the demands of the clan, the weight of responsibility and expectation. It had grown worse since what happened to Duncan, his elder brother.

"Ye are talking nonsense, woman," Quinn growled. "Ye know nothing about me."

"Don't I? I know this, Quinn MacFarlane. Ye will soon have a choice to make. Make the right one and ye could have yer heart's desire. Mayhap then ye'll stop searching. Mayhap then ye'll be happy instead of weighed down with guilt."

Quinn opened his mouth for an angry retort. How dare this woman preach at him? She knew nothing about him! But one look at the expression on her face stopped him. Her hard stare seemed to see right into his soul. He swallowed.

"Who are ye?" he whispered.

Irene MacAskill tossed the grouse bones into the fire then climbed to her feet. "A friend. Perhaps ye'll realize that at the end. Remember what I've told ye. Make the right choice."

With that she turned and disappeared into the night.

Quinn scrambled to his feet and called after her. He grabbed a burning brand from the fire and went searching all around the camp. There was no sign of Irene MacAskill.

Darcy sped along the winding road, letting her hair stream out behind her. She'd splashed out and hired a convertible and she was glad of it. The sensation of cruising along with the wind in her hair, the hills of the Highlands on one side, a gleaming loch on the other, was exhilarating.

Irene MacAskill's guide book lay on the passenger seat beside her. The strange woman had marked some places in the book and Darcy had decided to visit a few of them. She couldn't quite explain why. She just somehow felt it was the right thing to do.

The conference had ended last night. Darcy had called Gretchen and told her she wouldn't be home for a week or so. She was going to follow her friend's advice and take some time out. Gretchen was pleased, of course, and made Darcy promise to bring her back a bottle of authentic scotch whisky.

This morning Darcy had checked out of her hotel, hired a car and set out. She hadn't booked a hotel or planned an itinerary. She'd just driven; following the route Irene MacAskill had marked and seen what she found when she arrived. Having no plan, no destination in mind was oddly liberating.

Glancing to her left Darcy looked out over the loch. Fishing boats bobbed on its surface and on the far side Darcy spotted a village. Maybe she'd go visit. That was the beauty of having no plan. She could go exactly where her whims took her.

Darcy slowed for the bend ahead. She grabbed the gear stick and the gears crunched horribly as she changed down. She'd still not gotten used to right-hand drive or the gears.

"Damn it!" she muttered, fighting furiously with the gear stick.

She looked up and nearly had a heart attack when she saw a deer standing directly in her path. Darcy screamed, slammed her foot against the brake pedal and swerved. There was a thump and for one terrifying moment the car spun sideways before coming to a halt in a screech of tires.

Heart thumping Darcy threw open the car door and scrambled out. She looked around wildly. The deer was just disappearing over a rise. Darcy couldn't tell if it was injured but she assumed it must be.

"Oh god," she muttered. "Oh god."

She ran around to the trunk of the car and pulled out her medical bag. Then she took off after the deer. The vet in her was screaming that she must help the poor creature. She only hoped she'd be able to do so.

She reached the rise where she'd last seen the deer and saw it ambling along the loch shore. Darcy scrambled down the hillside, slipping and sliding most of the way until she reached the beach. A little further along the hillsides became steep cliffs and Darcy saw that one of them formed a natural stone arch that arced over the shore and into the waters of the loch.

The deer stood on the other side, looking back at her.

Darcy approached slowly. She didn't want to spook it. The deer didn't look injured but Darcy knew wild animals were good at hiding injuries. It was a survival technique to fool predators.

"Easy," Darcy murmured as she walked slowly closer. "I won't hurt you. I just want to check you're okay."

The deer watched her with large, liquid eyes. Its nose twitched, testing the air. Darcy had almost reached it when the creature bounded away along the beach.

Darcy cursed under her breath. She glanced up at the archway looming over her. There was something about it that seemed familiar. Was this marked in Irene MacAskill's guidebook?

It didn't matter. On the other side, Darcy's patient was getting away.

Darcy took a deep breath and stepped through the arch.

Chapter 3

As she stepped through the archway, something caught her foot and she stumbled, skidding to her knees on the sand. With a grumbled curse, she climbed to her feet and brushed off her jeans. There was a small tear on her right leg.

"Great," she murmured. "Just perfect!"

She turned in a slow circle. The deer was nowhere in sight. It obviously neither wanted nor needed her help. She'd done what she could. Time to return to the hire car and hope it wasn't too badly damaged.

Glancing to her right at the loch, Darcy noticed that the fishing boats had disappeared. Then she noticed something else: the settlement she'd seen on the far side of the loch was no longer there.

Odd, Darcy thought.

Darcy turned around to retrace her steps. But as she took a step to return through the archway, she realized that water now filled the area underneath it. Before there had been a thin strip of shoreline but now the archway rose straight out of the water and Darcy couldn't see the bottom.

What's going on? she thought. *The loch isn't tidal. Why had the water level changed like that?*

Whatever the explanation, it was clear that she wouldn't be returning that way. She had no idea of the water's depth and it would be just her luck to end up getting a dunking.

There *was* a path in front of her, however. There was still a strip of shoreline leading up to the low cliffs that ringed the shore. The path turned left from her position and climbed one of those cliffs in a switch-back trail.

With a shrug she started on the path, hoping she'd be able to double back to the car. She soon realized it was much steeper than it appeared. In places she was forced to scrabble on all fours, grabbing fistfuls of heather to help pull her up. By the time she reached the top she was puffing and panting. Her medical bag had never felt so heavy.

She straightened, looking around. There was no sign of the road or her car. Darcy frowned. Had she gotten turned around somehow? Surely her sense of direction wasn't that bad? She began hiking, hoping to hit the road.

But she didn't.

Twenty minutes passed and Darcy saw nothing and nobody. She stopped. If she carried on wandering like this, she would just get herself more lost.

"Okay, time to admit defeat," she muttered.

She pulled her cell phone from her bag and was about to dial the local police when she noticed the icon in the top right corner of the screen flashing to show there was no signal.

"Wonderful!" Darcy cried, throwing up her hands.

She held the cell phone up as high as possible and walked around the hilltop, trying to find a signal. It was no good. Her phone was useless.

She fought down a sudden surge of panic. Okay, so she was in the middle of nowhere with no path in sight. So what? This place was full of tourists so she was bound to come across someone eventually and she'd ask them for directions. In the meantime, she'd start following the line of the loch back the way she'd come. If she kept the loch on her left she would reach her car or find a road or something. Eventually.

Hefting her bag, she began walking. Her nostrils widened as she picked up an acrid scent wafting on the breeze. Wood smoke. She searched for its source and spotted a thin plume of smoke up ahead. She also heard the hum of conversation. With relief, she hurried on towards the smoke, hoping she'd stumbled across some campers who would let her use their phone, or even better, give her a lift back to her car.

She topped a rise and found herself looking down into a sheltered dell. On one side a small fire burned. Something was cooking on a pit over the fire – a rabbit by the looks of it – and three men were seated cross-legged round the fire talking quietly.

Darcy waved. "Hello! Sorry to interrupt your lunch."

The men looked up sharply. They seemed to be wearing traditional Scottish dress – a long plaid wrap over brown pants and soft leather boots. Maybe it was designed to impress tourists. They could wear evening dresses and tiaras for all Darcy cared, just as long as they let her use their phone.

"Sorry to startle you," she said. "But I've gotten myself a bit lost." She held up her cell phone and waved it at them. "I can't get a signal. Could I borrow your phone?"

The men looked at each other with puzzled expressions. Then one of them slowly climbed to his feet. He was tall and heavily muscled. Black hair hung to his shoulders in matted tangles. He had a huge sword strapped to his waist.

Darcy licked her lips. Probably plastic, that's all. A replica to add authenticity to his costume. These guys were obviously part of some kind of tourist attraction. That would explain their clothes and weapons. Yes, that must be it.

"What do you want, lass?" the man called.

"To use your phone," Darcy repeated. "Unless you can give me directions to the road? I left my car but can't find it again! Stupid of me, I know, but I'm new to these parts."

The man frowned. He glanced at his companions who shrugged. "Have ye suffered a knock on the head, woman? Yer words make nae sense to me."

Darcy paused, taken aback. "I'm sorry?"

The man craned his head to look behind Darcy. "Where are yer companions? This is a dangerous place to be out alone."

Dangerous? What was he talking about?

"Look, I think we've got crossed wires here. I just want to use your phone. But if you haven't got one that's fine. I'll just be on my way."

"I havenae got any wires, crossed or otherwise, although why ye should need it I canna ken," the man replied. "Where are yer kin folk?"

"My kin folk? You mean my family? Why do you want to know that?"

She took a few steps back. She was starting to regret approaching these men. She didn't like the way they were watching her. The two by the fire were leering and nudging each other in a way that sent a tingle of alarm down her spine.

"It's not safe for a woman to be out on her own in these parts. Not without her men-folk to protect her. So I wonder: what brings ye to our fire? Perhaps ye've come looking for us to warm ye up, eh?"

His companions grinned. "I know just how to warm this one up," one of the men said, rubbing his groin.

Panic spiked through Darcy. Yes, this had definitely been a bad idea. She spun around and sprinted but she'd only gone three steps when strong fingers grabbed her wrist and yanked her around. The black-haired man pulled her against him, pinning her arms against his chest.

"Where do ye think yer going in such a hurry?" he asked. "Don't yer ken it's impolite to turn down our offer of hospitality?"

"Let me go!" Darcy yelled. She pulled back her leg and kicked him in the shin as hard as she could.

The man grunted in pain but he didn't loosen his grip. With a growl of annoyance he dragged her down the hill towards the campfire. Darcy yelled and screamed, hoping somebody nearby would hear and come running to her aid. This only seemed to amuse the men more.

"Ye can scream yer heart out, lass. There's nobody here but us. The MacFarlanes are the only clan nearby and they are too far away to help ye."

He dragged her into the circle around the campfire and pushed her roughly to her knees. She landed heavily, her knees smacking into the hard rock that was only just below the surface of the soil. One of the men loomed over her. He pulled her bag from her grasp and tossed it away.

"Are you crazy?" Darcy yelled at him. "What the hell are you doing? Let me go, you asshole!" She surged to her feet and aimed another kick at the man.

He danced out of her reach and laughed. "Yer a fiery one, aren't ye? Sit down, be quiet and you'll nae be harmed. Carry on like this and I'll tie ye up and gag ye besides."

Darcy fought down her panic and forced herself to think. She could try to run. But there were three of them and only one of her, they'd probably catch her before she'd gone more than a few meters. She could scream for help. But that hadn't helped so far and she had no doubt he would follow through with his threat of gagging her. No, she needed to keep calm. She needed to think.

Raising her chin, she glared at the man. "What are you going to do with me?"

"Well, that's the question isn't it?" the man replied.

"Let's have some fun with her, Hamish," one of the men said. "She's asking for it. Why else would a woman be out here on her own?"

"Quiet, Conn," Hamish growled. "Yer not paid to think, remember? We'll nae lay a hand on her. Lord John will want this one, especially if she's some runaway from the MacFarlanes. We'll take her to him and let him decide what to do with her."

Conn paled a little, obviously afraid of this Lord John but was persistent. "Damn Lord John! He sends us out on these raids for days at a time with nae a warm bed or a warm woman in sight. How will he know if we have a bit of fun with her?"

Hamish lunged forward and landed a punch to Conn's face that snapped his head to the side. "Fool! Ye want to risk his wrath for a quick roll with some wench? Have ye forgotten what happened to Sean? You'll nae lay a hand on her, is that clear?"

Conn rubbed his cheek where a red welt was appearing and glared at Hamish sullenly. "Aye. Whatever ye say."

Darcy stared in horror at the three men. Their casual violence made her stomach churn. What the hell had she stumbled into? Was this some kind of criminal gang? If so, why were they out here miles from anywhere? None of this made any sense. But one thing was clear: for now she'd have to go along with what they wanted. If she didn't, she'd get hurt.

"Okay," she breathed. "I'll do what you want."

Hamish nodded. "Wise choice." He jerked his head at the other two. "Get packed up and put that fire out. Time we got moving. We don't want the MacFarlanes turning up looking for their lost sheep." He grinned suddenly. "They'll be mighty angry when they find we've captured one of their own. Lord John will most likely give us a reward."

This seemed to please the men. They scrambled to their feet and began gathering up their meager possessions. One of them wrapped the remaining meat in a piece of cloth and kicked soil over the fire. In moments they were ready to move.

Hamish pushed Darcy ahead of him and she managed to grab her bag and hold it against her chest. She went meekly as they left the dell, trying her best to seem subdued and compliant. She'd learned from her years as a vet that when surrounded by predators it was better to appear submissive. But inside, she felt anything but submissive. She was seriously pissed off. Who the hell did these men think they were?

The very first person or car she saw she intended to run off yelling and have the police pick these assholes up and throw the book at them. And if they didn't happen across anyone who could help her? Well, she'd just have to help herself.

She was going to escape.

Chapter 4

Quinn MacFarlane shifted his weight. He'd been lying on his elbows on top of the hillock for so long that his arms and shoulders were starting to go numb. The coarse heather kept scratching his skin through his plaid and the hot summer sun was making beads of sweat run down his forehead and dampen the shoulder-length braids he wore at the front of his raven-dark hair.

He'd found the brigands. They sat in the dell below, oblivious to Quinn watching them from above. Fools, the three of them. But dangerous fools nonetheless.

Quinn took out his quill and ink and scratched some more letters into the parchment, descriptions of the three men along with everything he'd been able to figure out since he'd started following their trail again this morning.

He frowned, rubbing at the two-day-old stubble that covered his chin. He was sure these brigands were the men he'd been looking for. So far they'd only taken live-stock and burned a few outbuildings but Quinn's brother, Laird Robert MacFarlane, was concerned that they would get bolder unless something was done about it.

Quinn shared his concerns. Coming this far south was a risky tactic. It took him mighty close to their neighbors, the Murrays, and there was no love lost between the two clans. But it was a risk he must take.

The three men had settled down in the lee of the hill. One of them started a fire and they'd begun cooking the rabbit they'd snared earlier. They seemed confident, relaxed, totally unaware that Quinn was watching them.

Quinn frowned. Something didn't fit. The men looked well fed and carried weapons that had recently been sharpened. They didn't look like the average brigand living in the wild and preying on travelers.

Quinn felt sure there was more to this. Somebody else, somebody powerful and with a grudge against the MacFarlanes was supplying these people with weapons and resources.

The brigands had mentioned a Lord John. Could it be John de Clare?

Will I never be free of that man? Quinn thought. *Has he not done enough with taking Duncan from us? Must he still plague my family?*

Quinn felt his body tense and forced himself to relax. It did no good thinking about that now. He had to focus on the task in hand.

He was just close enough that he could make out the men's muttered conversation. He strained his ears trying to pick up anything that would hint at their plans but they seemed to be bickering over who should cut up the rabbit.

"Hello?" a voice suddenly called from below.

Quinn turned his head to see a young woman approaching the dell. She'd come from the direction of the loch. " Hello! Sorry to interrupt your lunch."

Where had she come from? Quinn had scouted the area for miles around and there'd been no sign of a soul. She wore a shirt that hugged her figure in a way that was hardly decent, and trews that clung to her legs and seemed to be made of a thick blue material. She carried a leather bag and kept waving a small black object at the three brigands.

What was the lass doing? Had she lost her wits? Didn't she know brigands when she saw them? And what, by God, was she doing out here alone?

One of the brigands stood and approached the woman. Quinn listened tensely to their conversation although he couldn't understand much of what the woman was asking. Cell phone? Car? These were words Quinn didn't recognize. She must be a foreigner, a Sassenach perhaps, who didn't know their language too well.

And also didn't grasp the danger she'd put herself in.

Then suddenly the brigand grabbed the woman. In only moments he'd ripped the bag from her hands and pushed her roughly into the grass. Quinn was on his feet in an instant. The lass needed his help! He spun around and sprinted over to where he'd tethered Silver. He grabbed his bow from where it was tied to the saddle.

When he returned, the brigands had packed up their camp and were pushing the woman ahead of them from the dell.

Quinn quickly nocked an arrow and stood up so he was outlined against the sky. "Hold!" he bellowed. "Stay right where ye are!"

The men spun around, drawing their weapons.

"Let the lass go!" Quinn yelled.

"Piss off!" one of the brigands yelled back. "This is none of yer concern!"

Quinn released the string. His arrow sped towards its target, punching into the man's shoulder. With a yelp he dropped his sword and toppled to the ground where he lay writhing. The other brigands started towards him, yelling.

"Run, lass!" he bellowed. "Run!"

But she didn't.

Instead she grabbed her bag and swung it with all her might. It connected with the side of one of the brigand's head and knocked him out cold. That left one man standing - the leader. With a growl Quinn nocked a third arrow. But the man was stalking the woman and was too close - if he fired down he risked hitting her.

The lass backed up a few steps, holding the bag in front of her like a shield as the man approached.

"Ye'll pay for that!" he growled.

The woman suddenly dropped the bag, bent and pulled an object from inside. As the last brigand lunged for her, she whipped her arm towards his neck. Quinn saw something flash and then the brigand's hand flew to his neck.

"What did ye do?" he spat. "I'm gonna-"

He didn't finish the sentence. His legs went weak and he toppled face-first to the ground. The woman stared at the three downed brigands, her eyes wide with fear. Then she glanced up at Quinn standing on the hilltop.

Then she ran.

With a curse Quinn sprinted to his horse. He swung up into the saddle and kicked the black gelding into an urgent gallop.

He didn't blame the girl for fleeing. She didn't know that Quinn was trying to help her. For all she knew he might be one of the brigands. But he couldn't let her go running off into the hills alone. She was confused and frightened. Anything could happen to her.

He galloped down the hill. In her fright she'd made no effort to hide her tracks and her trail was easily visible in the trampled heather and footprints of her flight.

Quinn thundered over the ground, the wind sending his hair streaming out behind him. His eyes scanned the terrain, searching. She might have taken cover, trying to hide from him. He topped a rise and saw her up ahead. She was sprinting like she had the very devil on her tail. She held that strange little black box in her hand and was jabbing at it desperately with the fingers of one hand.

"Hold, lass!" he shouted. "I'll nae harm ye!"

She glanced over her shoulder and her eyes widened in terror. She redoubled her pace, pelting over the rough terrain without a thought for the obstacles that might catch her ankle and easily break a leg.

Quinn cursed. He urged the horse to greater speed. He overtook her and spun his mount around, intending to block her way but she merely swerved and went running off in the other direction.

Quinn kicked one foot out of his stirrup and then flung his leg over the saddle, jumping from the animal. He hit the ground and rolled, already running as he came back to his feet. He pelted after her.

She was fast but he was faster. Years of training and daily practice meant Quinn could run like this for hours if need be. He caught her just as she reached a clump of scraggly brush and stretched a hand to her shoulder.

"Stop, lass!"

She spun and her fist connected with his chin. "Leave me alone, you asshole!"

Then she was off again. Quinn rubbed his chin and took off after her. He was more than a little annoyed now. Did the lass not realize he was trying to help her? Had he not already said he meant her no harm?

This time he launched himself, grabbing her around the waist and taking them both crashing to the ground among the springy heather. She screamed - more in fury than fear Quinn thought - and fought like a wildcat. She punched and kicked and writhed and it was all Quinn could do to stop himself sustaining injury.

"Calm down, woman!" he yelled as they tussled amongst the heather. "I'm not going to hurt ye! I swear!"

He managed to grab her wrists and pin them to the ground on either side of her head. He straddled her chest and held her fast.

"Stop! I'm tired of getting hit by a bloody woman!"

The lass stopped struggling but she stared up at Quinn with defiance in her eyes. She was trembling and Quinn felt a sudden stab of guilt. It was no wonder she'd attacked him - he'd gone pelting after her like a mad man.

"My name is Quinn," he said in the same soothing voice he used with a spooked horse. "Quinn MacFarlane. I'm nae gonna hurt ye. Ye have my word. I'm not one of those brigands, lass. I've come to help ye."

She didn't reply. She just stared up at him, unblinking. My, but she was a beauty. She had olive skin and deep brown eyes like freshly turned soil. Her dark hair spread out in waves around her head. Where had she come from? And why did she behave so strangely?

"I'm gonna let ye up now but ye must give me yer word you willnae try to run again. It's nae safe for a woman to be wandering these hills alone."

"All right!" she cried. "I won't run. Just let me up!"

Quinn climbed to his feet and the woman scrambled up after him, backing away down the trail. She still held the little glass thing in her hand, he noticed. Her bag lay off to the side amongst the heather.

"Ye could have stuck me with that thing the same as ye did with those brigands, lass. Why did ye not?"

She glanced at the glass thing and shrugged. "It's horse tranquilizer. Not enough to do any damage but it will keep him asleep for an hour or two. Do you have a phone? I need to call the police."

Quinn cocked his head. None of her words made any sense. "I didnae ken the least bit of what ye said, lass. Are ye speaking some foreign tongue? I didnae recognize half the words."

She stared at him as if he'd gone mad. Then she shook her head. "This is crazy," she muttered to herself. "Crazy." She dragged a hand down her face and pulled in a breath. "I didn't stick you with this because you shot that man and freed me. I guessed you weren't with them."

"Then why did ye run from me?"

"Are you kidding? A hulking guy in a Scottish fancy dress costume starts chasing me and you expect me not to run? What the hell is going on here? Who were those men? Who are you? What do you want?"

Quinn held up his hand. "Whoa, lass. Which question would ye like me to answer first? I told ye who I am. Quinn MacFarlane, brother to Laird Robert MacFarlane. Those three were brigands who've been raiding our outlying holdings. I was tracking them when ye came upon them. As for what I want with ye - nothing, lass. Only to see ye safe."

She blinked and then abruptly slid to a cross-legged position on the ground. With a groan, she pressed the heels of her hands against her forehead. "I was only out for a drive," she said. "I just wanted to see a bit of Scotland before I flew home. How can this have happened? It's like something out of a freaking horror movie!"

"Out of a what?"

She laughed. It was a little shrill, like she was on the edge of hysteria. "Let me guess - you haven't heard of horror movies?"

Quinn shook his head.

"Or the police? Or cell phones? Jesus, where have you been living? In a cave?"

"Ye shouldnae take the Lord's name in vain," Quinn scolded her. "And no, I havenae been living in a cave. I live in Dunbreggan, the seat of my clan, up by the mouth of the loch."

This didn't seem to reassure her. She squeezed her eyes shut and began taking deep breaths as if to calm herself. He squatted in front of her but didn't draw any closer. She was like a startled animal - one wrong move and she'd bolt again.

"Where are ye from, lass? Where are ye kin? If I can get ye back to them I will."

"I'm from America," she said, waving a hand when he gave her a puzzled look. "Don't worry about it. It's a long way away, over the ocean. I was at a conference in Edinburgh when I hit a deer. Listen, could you take me to a police station? I need to get my car back."

There she went again, using words he'd never heard. Maybe they were words used in this 'America'. He'd heard tales of such a place over the sea that the Spanish had discovered but didn't know of anyone from that land traveling to Europe.

"I'm sorry, lass," he said, shaking his head. "But I've never heard of this 'Police Station'. Be that a keep? To which clan does it belong?"

"It doesn't belong to anyone," she said. "It's a place where the local police are based - you know, constables, lawkeepers, whatever the hell you call them over here. They'll have a phone! My god, I need a phone!"

Quinn ignored her taking the Lord's name in vain again. She had an odd way of speaking. Maybe it was normal in America. "Well I canna take you back to this Police Station for I dinna ken where it might lie. Nor can I leave you here. It's nae safe. Ye'll have to come with me till we can figure out what's to be done with ye."

"Come with you?" she said. "Come with you where?"

"To the keep where my brother is laird. He's a wise man. He'll know how to help ye."

She scrambled to her feet. She looked wary again, ready to run. "How do I know I can trust you?"

"I give ye my word ye'll nae come to any harm whilst yer under my protection, lass."

This didn't seem to convince her. What kind of place was this America where a man's word meant nothing to a woman?

Her eyes moved to something behind him and Quinn turned to see, Silver, his black gelding coming towards him. The animal, although well trained, was incredibly greedy. True to form, tufts of grass stuck out each side of his mouth as he munched.

"You shouldn't let him eat that," the woman said. "He'll get colic."

The sudden shift in conversation threw him a little. "Ye know about horses?"

"Yes. I'm a veterinarian. That's why I was at the conference in Edinburgh."

Quinn laughed, shaking his head. "Lass, yer gonna have to stop talking like that or else write down the meaning of half the words ye say."

The woman frowned. "You don't know what a veterinarian is? Um," she pursed her lips in thought. "A doctor. A healer. One that looks after animals."

Quinn had never heard of such a thing but at least she was talking instead of trying to run or fight. Progress.

"Well, be that as it may, I'd like to see ye try to keep Silver from eating whatever he likes. He's a headstrong beast and no mistake." He turned towards the horse, put his fingers to his lips and let out two short, shrill whistles. Silver pricked up his ears and then trotted over, gently nuzzling Quinn's hands, hoping for a treat.

The woman watched him, a slightly puzzled expression on her face as if she was surprised he'd be so gentle with his horse. Quinn had to force himself not to frown. People often misjudged him because of his size and his skill at fighting. Why would this woman be any different, particularly considering the circumstances of their meeting?

"Do ye have a name, lass?" he asked.

She bit her lip as if deciding whether to answer. Then she stuck out her hand. "I'm Darcy. Darcy Greenway."

Quinn took her hand and kissed the back of it. "Very pleased to make yer acquaintance, Lady Greenway."

Darcy seemed taken aback. "I..um..I...."

Her hand felt soft and warm in his. It was so tiny his fingers enfolded it easily. "Will ye agree to accompany me back to my clan's holdings, my lady? We can protect ye there until we can figure out how to get ye back to Edinburgh and yer kin."

Darcy pulled her hand from his. She took a few steps backwards, looking around as if for escape.

"I give ye my word I'll do ye nae harm nor will any member of my clan. Yer under my protection now." He drew his dagger and held it out to her, hilt-first. "And just in case ye doubt me, ye can have my dagger. You'll ride behind me on Silver and if I do anything ye dinna like ye can stick me with the knife. I canna say fairer than that."

Darcy reached out and hesitantly took the knife. It was an ornate thing, given to him by his brother, Robert, for his nameday.

"Quinn," she said his name as though trying it out on her tongue. "Can I ask you something?" She swallowed, seeming to gather her courage. "What year is this?"

"Year?" Had the lass taken a whack on the head? Had those ruffians hurt her more than he realized? "It's the year of Our Lord 1505," he said gently.

She turned pale. Her legs folded beneath her and she would have fallen if Quinn hadn't darted forward to catch her. She weighed next to nothing in his arms, like a fragile little bird.

"Are ye well, lass? Are ye hurt?"

She shook her head. "No. I'm fine. I just felt a bit weird for a minute there."

But she made no move to pull out of his grip and Quinn didn't let her go. Instead, before she could protest, he scooped her up and lifted her into Silver's saddle. He tied her bag to the side of the saddle and then swung up in front of her.

"Ye'll need to put yer arms around my waist," he told her. "I dinna want ye falling off and we have a long way to go."

She did as he instructed, resting her hands lightly on his hips. Well, it was a start.

"Do ye still have the dagger, lass?" he asked.

"I sure do," Darcy replied. "So you better not try anything."

That was more like it. More like the feisty little thing who'd fought off him and the brigands.

"I wouldnae dream of it."

They set off at a steady walk. Quinn would have liked to go faster – those brigands might have come around by now – but he was afraid of jostling the lass too much or scaring her all over again. He scanned the area as they moved, searching for any sign of their enemies. Thankfully, there were none. This area, so close to the border of their lands was sparsely populated. The lass said nothing. Her hands were a reassuring touch against his hips and he could feel her presence at his back like a warm summer heat.

Quinn gritted his teeth in determination. He'd see her safely back to the clan and then he'd find a way to return her to her kin. She was under his protection and nobody was going to harm her.

Chapter 5

This was crazy. Completely crazy. Darcy was damned sure she must be losing her mind. Either that or she'd stumbled on some weird sect that chose to dress in medieval costume and give up all the trappings of modern life. It must be that. The alternative was too crazy to think about.

Think it through, she told herself. *You're a scientist. Rationalize this.*

In her experience the simplest explanation was normally the correct one. But that would mean Quinn was telling the truth and this really was 1505. Somehow she had been transported back in time over five hundred years.

"Are ye all right, lass?" Quinn asked.

His large, strong hands held the reins lightly and he swayed to the movements of the horse. He seemed completely at ease in the saddle as if he had been riding all his life. This close he smelt of wood smoke and leather with a faint trace of masculine sweat no doubt garnered through his pursuits of her.

"I-" Darcy began.

What the hell was she supposed to say to that question? *Yeah, I'm absolutely dandy, thanks. I'm thousands of miles from home, hundreds of years from home, riding with a strange man, in a strange land, and I think I might be losing my mind.*

Quinn seemed to sense her unease. "Tell me what happened to ye, lass. How did ye run into those brigands in the first place?"

Okay. She could do that. "Like I said, I was in my car when I got out to find a deer I hit. I'm a vet, I wanted to help it. Then suddenly everything was...different. I couldn't find my car. I stumbled into those men and thought they might have a phone I could use." She shivered at the memory of the violence she saw in their eyes. "I never expected them to be such assholes."

"By this word 'assholes' I ken ye mean malefactors, and aye, they were certainly that. Twas' bad luck that you ran into them in the first place. I hope ye dinna think all of us highlanders are like that."

Darcy didn't reply. She was so confused she didn't know what to think. In the space of an hour she'd been attacked, imprisoned, freed, and rescued. It was like something out of a bad B-movie.

"Well," she said at last. "I guess I'll find out when we reach your house, won't I?"

As they traveled steadily north, the wildness began to be replaced by small crofts dotted with sheep and Highland cattle with their distinctive long hair. Cottages started to appear, most with walled off gardens at the front that housed coops of chickens and herds of honking geese. Guard dogs pricked up their ears and watched them pass and a few times the crofters waved to Quinn and called out greetings.

The sun was starting to sink when Quinn pulled Silver to a halt at the top of a rise. Darcy stretched her neck, looking over Quinn's shoulder.

She gasped at the sight that greeted her.

Below, on the shores of the loch lay a village. It was bordered on one side by the loch itself which sparkled in the evening sunlight and on the other side by undulating purple hills covered in heather. On the other side of the loch Darcy could see the hills rising up to snow-capped mountains in the distance. An island rose from the center of the loch and on this island perched a castle with high walls and turrets where a flag flew in the breeze. The castle was connected to the mainland by a causeway and Darcy could see a steady stream of people and horses moving along that causeway. It was a stunning vista and Darcy stared, transfixed, taking it all in.

Quinn seemed pleased by her reaction. "Welcome to Dunbreggan," he said. "Seat of clan MacFarlane." He nudged Silver into a walk. "If we've timed it right, we should have arrived just in time for the evening meal. I don't know about ye, lass, but I'm so hungry I could eat a horse."

"Maybe not a horse," Darcy replied. "But a hamburger and fries would be very welcome."

As they rode down the hillside, the people stopped what they were doing and shouted greetings to Quinn. Many were dressed in warrior's garb, wearing long plaid wrapped around their tall frames and carrying huge swords strapped to their back. These greeted Quinn with good-hearted banter, asking what was this treasure he'd found on his travels.

Darcy blushed but Quinn seemed unperturbed, answering them with banter of his own which amounted to telling them to mind their own business. Still others, dressed as common villagers seemed excited at Quinn's return and shouted respectful greetings and blessings for his good health. Quinn answered them all by name and tossed a few coins to the excited children who gathered to follow the horse.

Darcy watched it all in silence. She felt an odd mix of emotions. She was relieved to be amongst people again - people who appeared friendly and welcoming, but at the same time was keenly aware of the curiosity with which everyone regarded her. Nobody said anything but she could see from their stares that they had many questions. Who was she? Why had Quinn brought her back here? Why was she dressed so strangely?

Darcy had never liked being the center of attention and she cringed, trying to hide behind Quinn's broad back.

They made their way through the village and onto the causeway. At last they reached the gates to the castle. The walls were high and thick, a defensive measure, but to Darcy it made the whole thing look like some beast that was about to swallow her up.

A teenage lad came running to take the horse as they pulled up inside the gates. Quinn swung effortlessly out of the saddle and then reached up to help Darcy down. She all but fell into his arms, stiff from the ride and shaky from the day's experiences. His arms went around her, catching her easily and setting her on her feet. He held her a moment longer than was necessary and she found herself looking up at his shockingly handsome face. She was trapped in the circle of his arms but she didn't feel trapped. She felt...safe. Quinn's eyes were intense as he watched her and she couldn't tell what he was thinking.

Then he seemed to remember where he was. He cleared his throat and released her, stepping back.

"Colm, see that Silver is rubbed down well, he's had a hard day. Give him an extra bag of oats tonight."

The lad nodded and sketched an awkward bow. "Aye, Quinn. I'll see it done." He hovered, flicking a glance at Darcy, obviously full of questions.

"Well?" Quinn said. "Hop to it, lad. Has nobody ever told ye tis rude to stare at a lady?"

Colm jumped. "Aye. Sorry." He took Silver's reins and led him away.

Quinn watched him go with a frown on his face. "That lad will be a heart-breaker before long, I've nae doubt," he said. "Perhaps it's time we thought about finding him a wife."

A wife? Darcy thought. *What the hell? That boy couldn't be more than sixteen!*

"Come, lass, let's go introduce ye to my family."

Darcy nodded, little butterflies swirling in her stomach. How would they receive her? Would they be as kind as Quinn? Or would they resent this stranger coming into their midst?

She took the arm that Quinn held out to her and allowed him to lead her to the main doors of the keep.

A woman waited for them on the steps. She looked to be around Darcy's age, with long red hair failing in a braid to her waist and a belly swollen with the later stages of pregnancy.

"Och, Quinn!" she cried as they approached. "There ye are! We were expecting ye back hours ago. Where have ye been?"

Quinn folded the woman into an embrace and gave her a kiss on the cheek. Darcy was shocked by the sudden stab of jealousy that assailed her. Was this his wife?

"Rebecca, ye always worry, nae matter how long we might be away."

"That's because I know how ye men like to get yerselves into trouble!" she said, scowling. "Perhaps if ye took more care I'd not have to worry so much, ye ken?"

"Aye. Point taken but ye know I have to do these patrols, especially with the raids we've been having."

The woman sighed. "I ken it, I do. So what did ye find on yer patrol, Quinn? More than ye bargained for by the looks of things."

Quinn nodded. "Aye, ye could say that." He turned to Darcy. "This is Lady Darcy Greenway, a visitor to our lands from across the ocean. Lady Greenway, I'd like ye to meet Rebecca MacFarlane, wife to my brother, Laird Robert."

She was his sister-in-law? A strange wave of relief washed through Darcy. What was she doing? She'd only known Quinn for a few hours!

"Lady Greenway was set upon by three brigands down near the border. She managed to free herself mind, so I thought it best to bring her here till we can figure out how to get her back to her kin."

Rebecca's hands flew to her mouth and she looked at Darcy with an expression of horror. Then, to Darcy's surprise, she pulled her into a tight embrace, hampered somewhat by Rebecca's bump.

"Och! Ye poor dear. Whatever must ye think of my countrymen? Yer first visit to our bonny land and ye stumble upon the worst of men!"

She seemed to take it as a personal affront. Darcy returned the hug a little awkwardly until Rebecca stepped back and looked her over critically.

Rebecca was pretty with large eyes and a dusting of freckles over her nose. "Are ye well?" she asked Darcy. "Did they hurt ye?"

"No," Darcy replied. "In fact, I think I hurt them more than they hurt me in the end."

Rebecca's eyes widened and she glanced at Quinn. "Ye mean ye fought them off?"

Darcy shrugged. "I drugged them actually, but it had much the same effect."

The look that crossed Rebecca's face suggested she was as puzzled by Darcy's words as Quinn had been. A moment later though, Rebecca's smile returned.

"Well, ye dinna need to worry. Yer safe now. Won't ye come inside? The evening meal is about to be served."

"Rebecca," Quinn said, catching her by the wrist. "Is Robert back yet? We need to talk about these raids. They're getting bolder."

Rebecca looked troubled. "Nay, he's not back yet. He and Dougal rode over to the northern holdings this morning after reports came in of more cattle raids. I'm sure he won't be long and then ye men can sit down and plan strategy while us women talk of more pleasant things." She tried to sound light-hearted but Darcy heard the tension in her voice.

Rebecca took Darcy's arm and led her through the doors. Beyond lay a huge hall with a beamed ceiling, flagstone floor covered by thick rugs and tapestries covering the walls. A huge fireplace sat against one wall although there was no fire burning in it now.

Darcy snapped her mouth shut when she realized she was staring. Long benches filled the room with a grand table at the far end. People of all ages sat at the benches, many already eating but others waiting to be served. The hum of conversation echoed through the room along with raucous laughter coming from a table populated by men dressed in warrior garb.

Quinn saw the men and scowled. "It doesnae take long for discipline to slip does it?"

Rebecca waved a hand at him. "Och, let them have their fun. They brought down a stag today over by the brook and so deserve to be in high spirits. We'll have venison for the next few days."

"Quinn!" one of the warriors shouted, standing up and saluting Quinn with his cup. "Come join us! Looks like yer day's hunting was as profitable as ours." He nodded meaningfully at Darcy.

"I'll thank ye to remember yer manners, Andrew MacFarlane," Quinn growled. "Especially when there are ladies present."

Andrew sobered abruptly. He bobbed a short bow to Rebecca and Darcy. "Of course. My apologies, my ladies."

Darcy shrank back behind Quinn. Many of the people in the hall had marked Quinn's entrance and now they were turning to look at the commotion.

Oh god, she thought. *They're all looking at me! I need to get out of here!*

She didn't realize she'd staggered until Quinn caught her by the elbow.

"What's wrong, lass? Ye look as pale as milk."

"I...er...um..." Darcy mumbled.

"Wouldn't ye feel a bit weakened if ye'd had the sort of day she's had?" Rebecca said, coming to Darcy's rescue. "Come on, my dear, we'll draw ye a bath, get ye some fresh clothing and then ye can come down to dinner when yer ready. Ye'll be right in no time, I'm sure."

Darcy nodded dumbly. Rebecca led her towards a staircase at the back of the room. Darcy realized Quinn wasn't following and looked back anxiously. Was he just going to leave her with strangers?

What are you talking about? she thought. *He's a stranger too. You've only known him a few hours!* And yet she'd grown reliant on him in that short time. She felt vulnerable without him by her side. She glanced over her shoulder, searching for him but he'd already turned away, dismissing her, and going over to speak to his men.

Darcy followed Rebecca up the stairs. At the top she found a long hallway with ornately carved doors along each side. Rebecca opened one of them and led Darcy into an opulent bedroom that wouldn't look out of place in some five star hotel. There was wood paneling on the wall, thick red and gold rugs covering the floor and a huge canopied bed dominating the space. An ornate fireplace sat against one wall.

"Oh my," Darcy said, looking around in wonder.

"Are ye all right, my dear?" Rebecca asked.

"Yes. It's this room. It's beautiful."

Rebecca fairly beamed at the compliment. "It's kind of ye to say so. Clan MacFarlane prides itself on treating our guests well. Ye'll want for nothing while yer here and ye'll be perfectly safe so try to nae worry about those brigands who beset ye."

"Thank you, Rebecca," Darcy said and meant it. She felt a sudden wave of gratitude for this woman who'd shown her such kindness. She nodded to Rebecca's swollen belly. "When are you due?"

Rebecca smiled, rubbing her stomach gently. "Another month or so the midwife reckons. I wish it would come sooner, tis starting to get mighty uncomfortable!"

Darcy laughed. "Are you having a boy or a girl?" As soon as the words left her lips, she regretted them. She really needed to learn to watch her tongue.

Rebecca looked at her, puzzled, then shrugged. "How would I know? Malcolm would dearly love a boy, I know, although he hasn't said as much. Me? I dinna care. As long as the bairn is healthy that's all that matters."

There was a knock at the door and a straw-haired girl stuck a head in. She bobbed a curtsy to Rebecca. "Begging yer pardon, but Quinn sent me up to bring the lady some clothes and water for bathing."

"Come in, Alice," Rebecca said, taking the girl by the hand.

She looked to be in her late teens and was a pretty little thing with a mischievous twinkle in her eyes. She smiled at Darcy.

"If it please ye, Lady Darcy, I'll help ye to bathe and change."

"Call me Darcy, please," Darcy said. Where had they all gotten the idea that she was a lady?

Alice nodded then turned to the door and called instructions into the corridor outside. Four young lads bustled into the room carrying a copper tub which they set before the fireplace and filled with hot water from buckets they'd brought with them.

After they'd left Rebecca took Darcy's hand. "Alice will take good care of ye. Come down to the hall when ye are ready. The weaver will be coming soon to show me some new material. You can help me pick out what I want for my gowns." She patted her belly. "Seems like I need a new gown every other week!"

She gave Darcy a quick kiss on the cheek and then left, closing the door softly behind her. Alice stuck her hand into the bathtub to test the water then tossed some powder in from a little box tied to her waist. The scent of lavender filled the room.

"Would ye like me to help ye undress?" Alice asked.

"Um, no," Darcy replied. "I've got it. Thanks."

Alice nodded and Darcy expected her to leave, allowing her to bathe in privacy, but Alice just stood there, hands clasped in front of her, watching Darcy expectantly.

Darcy swallowed. The bath really did look inviting. She walked over to the tub and undressed as quickly as she could, tossing her clothes onto the bed and then hopping into the bathtub and sinking gratefully into the hot water. She laid back, allowing the warmth of the water and the scent of lavender to unknot her tired muscles. Slowly, the tension left her.

She closed her eyes. It had been a crazy day. Crazy. Perhaps she was dreaming. Perhaps when she woke she'd be back in Edinburgh, or better, back in her apartment.

"It was a dream," she said aloud. "I've fallen asleep in the bath back home but I'm about to wake up."

"What was a dream, my lady?" Alice asked.

Startled, Darcy opened her eyes. Alice was kneeling by the side of the tub, sleeves of her gown rolled up, holding a bar of soap.

"Oh, nothing," Darcy muttered. "Ignore me. It's been a trying day."

"Would ye like me to scrub yer back?"

Darcy leaned forward, submitting herself to Alice's ministrations. She was glad she did. The girl had a deft touch which left Darcy feeling relaxed and refreshed.

Alice dried Darcy off and then presented her with a beautiful gown. It was a gorgeous thing in deep red velvet with gold scroll work around the bodice and the arms. Alice helped Darcy into it and once again she was glad of her help – she would never have been able to do up the hooks at the back by herself.

Alice led her over to the mirror where she brushed out Darcy's hair then pinned it up around her face, leaving several wisps framing her face and brushing her shoulder.

Standing back, Alice sighed. "Ye are a beauty my lady."

Darcy looked at herself in the mirror. She hardly recognized the person staring back. This wasn't Darcy Greenway, the jeans-and-t-shirt girl. This was a medieval princess, all grace and poise.

She giggled nervously. "What have you done to me, Alice? I barely recognize myself!"

Alice blushed. "I'm glad ye like it, my lady."

Darcy fixed her with a frown.

"Sorry. I mean, I'm glad ye like it, Darcy. Will ye go down to dinner now? I know Lady Rebecca will be waiting for ye."

Darcy pulled in a deep breath and let it out slowly, steeling her courage. Then she stood.

"Yes, thank you, Alice."

With as much confidence as she could muster she walked out the door and then along the corridor to the stairs. At the top she paused. The sounds of conversation had gotten louder and somebody was playing a fiddle.

Grabbing the railing with one hand, Darcy made her way down the steps. It was awkward walking in a gown and she feared she'd trip and go tumbling into the hall to land on her backside. She smiled at the thought. Wouldn't that be a way to introduce herself to the clan?

As she stepped into the hall she immediately looked for Quinn. There he was, sitting with his men at a table on the far side of the room. He looked up and she raised her hand to wave but halted as his eyes flicked over her and then away, dismissing her completely.

Darcy faltered, unsure of herself. What was she supposed to do? She needn't have worried. Rebecca, seated at the main table by the hearth, waved in Darcy's direction.

"Come join us, Lady Darcy," she called. "Ye can help me choose cloth for the bairn's swaddling."

Another woman sat with Rebecca. She had shiny black hair in a braid over her shoulder and looked to be only a few years older than Darcy. The woman smiled at Darcy encouragingly.

Feeling a little self-conscious, Darcy picked her way around the outside of the hall to Rebecca's table and sank gratefully into the seat she was offered.

"How are ye now, dear?" Rebecca asked. "Was the bath to yer liking?"

Darcy nodded. "I feel much better, thanks. It's amazing how a bath and a change of clothes can work wonders."

Rebecca laughed lightly. "Aye, it is that. And the gown? Ye look lovely as I'm sure the males in this room have noticed."

Darcy glanced around and noticed more than a few looks in her direction. She looked down, blushing. "It's a gorgeous dress, Rebecca. Thank you."

"Don't thank me, thank our Lily here." She nodded to the other woman. "Ye are wearing a gown she made me before I realized I was expecting. Lilly is our weaver and seamstress and she's single-handedly made our clan the envy of every woman in the Highlands."

Lily rolled her eyes at Rebecca and smiled. "It's nice to meet you, Lady Darcy. You'll have to forgive Rebecca, she's prone to a little exaggeration."

Lily had a different accent to the rest of them and it took Darcy a moment to place it. "You're English?"

"Aye, she's a Sassenach but she's all right all the same," Rebecca said, grinning at Lily.

"I grew up in London," Lily explained. "But came north when my father was posted to the garrison at Carlisle. The border has moved so many times, sometimes part of Scotland, sometimes part of England." She shrugged. "What are lines on a map? It's all the same to me."

"Our Lily would be the pride of the court should she ever choose to leave us," Rebecca said. "But she's decided to stay. I can't think why."

There was a mischievous look in Rebecca's eyes and Lily blushed. "Will you give over, Becca? You just love embarrassing me."

Rebecca laughed and squeezed Lily's shoulder. "And if I'm not very much mistaken, the reason for yer willingness to stay has just walked in."

Darcy glanced over to see a group of men striding through the doors. The man in front was tall and broad shouldered and dressed in fine clothing that set him a little apart from the rest.

Behind him came a group of warriors, heavily armed. Lily's eyes flicked to a man towards the back who had dark curly hair and a light dusting of stubble. The man looked up and smiled at Lily. The weaver, flustered, gave a tiny smile in response and then looked away.

Rebecca elbowed Darcy. "That's our Fraser, and Lily's beloved if only the two of them would have the courage to admit it! And that handsome fellow in front is my husband, Laird Robert."

Quinn rose from his seat and walked over to greet his brother. They clasped hands, forearm to forearm and slapped each other on the shoulder. They conferred quickly and then both turned to stride towards the head table. Darcy shrank back as they approached but Rebecca rose to her feet and moved around the table to greet her husband.

The big man scooped her up and gave her a long, passionate kiss. "Yer a sight for sore eyes, woman," he rumbled in a deep voice. "How's my wee one?" He ran his hand gently over Rebecca's bump.

"Kicking and squirming and being every bit as troublesome to me as his father is," Rebecca replied. "Let go of me ye big oaf, you stink of sweat and horse!"

Robert laughed and gave Rebecca a bow. "My apologies, my lady." He straightened and Darcy shifted uncomfortably as his eyes settled on her. He and Quinn were different in coloring. Robert had corn-yellow hair rather than dark, but they both shared the wide-shouldered physique and the penetrating blue eyes.

"Lady Darcy," Laird Robert said. "Quinn has briefly told me yer story. Be welcome in clan MacFarlane."

"I..." Darcy stammered. "Thank you, my lord."

Robert, Quinn and the rest of the men who'd arrived with Robert seated themselves at the table. A serving girl brought them ale and bread which they set to ravenously. Rebecca resumed her seat and began talking with Lily about different materials and clothes she wanted for the bairn.

Darcy listened with half an ear but her attention kept drifting to Quinn. He sat with Robert less than three paces from Darcy. He paid her no heed, instead supping on his ale and eating the food as if Darcy didn't even exist.

Why should I care? Darcy asked herself. *I don't even know him. I don't care if he ignores me. I don't.*

Chapter 6

Quinn was glad of the meal. Eating and drinking gave him something to focus his attention on, and, Lord, did he need it. He could feel Darcy's presence like she sat right next to him, even though she was down at the far end of the table. He kept glancing, hoping to find her looking back at him but every time he did she wasn't paying him any interest at all, instead she was deep in conversation with Rebecca and Lily.

He didn't know whether to be relieved or annoyed about that.

When Darcy walked into the hall earlier it had taken all of Quinn's willpower not to stare. The last thing the lass needed after what she'd gone through this day was him leering over her like some drooling brute. MacFarlane men were brought up better than that. They were taught to treat women with respect, not as though they were some trophy to be paraded around.

So, as Darcy entered the great hall, he'd been careful not to ogle her, no matter how much he'd wanted to. But it was hard. Lord, it was hard.

She was a beauty. Those huge brown eyes, so full of wit and intelligence. That long glossy hair. That diminutive figure that hid a feisty, wild spirit.

Quinn shook himself. What was he doing? He barely knew the lass. And she'd be leaving as soon as they found a way to return her to Edinburgh. With an effort, he forced his attention to what his brother was saying.

"Looks as though they're getting bolder," Robert said. "A large group attacked some of the northern holdings just yesterday. Burned out Aiden and Sarah's croft and left them for dead. It was pure good fortune that they got out with their bairns and managed to get to safety with Angus and Elspeth at the next croft."

Quinn felt anger rising inside him. These people were cowards to victimize crofters who had no way to defend themselves - the worst kind of men in Quinn's opinion.

"Did they take anything?" he asked.

"Aye, both their horses," Robert winced. "But ken this, they slaughtered what they couldnae take with them - all the chickens and as many of the geese as they could catch."

There was angry muttering around the table. Brigands stealing to survive was one thing but wanton slaughter for the sake of slaughter? That was just evil.

"Who were they?" Quinn asked. "Did Aiden or Sarah get a good look at them?"

Robert nodded. "Aye, they did. Enough to describe the bastards to us." He nodded to Matty who drew a rolled parchment from his cloak. "We've got their descriptions and we'll send it to every outlying village and outpost, telling them to keep watch. We'll catch these bastards, ye mark my words. Brigands and outlaws are lazy. They'll make a mistake sooner or later and when they do, we'll hunt them down like the animals they are."

The rest of the men nodded their agreement but Quinn found himself shaking his head.

"I dinna reckon it be that simple, brother."

"What do ye mean?"

"I've not yet told ye how I came upon the Lady Darcy today. I was tracking the brigands who attacked the south holding a few days back. They were heading south, towards the border of our land when the Lady Darcy stumbled into them. They took her prisoner but didnae lay a hand on her. They said they were taking her to their lord and mention a 'Lord John'."

That got their attention. Silence fell and Quinn could almost hear the men's thoughts tumbling.

"Ye think it might be John de Clare?" Robert said at last.

Quinn nodded. "It would be a mighty coincidence if it weren't. Ye know he swore vengeance against us and the rumors say he's married Laird Malcolm's daughter. If so, he'll be laird of the Murrays in all but name. Everyone knows how frail Laird Malcolm is. John de Clare will have the warriors of the Murray clan at his disposal to do with as he wishes. It would nae be hard to have them dress like common brigands and have them harry our lands."

The men shifted uncomfortably. Robert's hand curled around his ale cup so hard his knuckles went white.

"That bastard," he breathed. "Aye, I see it now. That would be just the type of underhanded thing he'd do."

"Why?" Fraser asked. The young warrior looked angry. He'd lost a good friend at the hands of John de Clare, just as Quinn and Robert had lost a brother. "Why would he raid us like this? If he wants vengeance why not just declare a feud and bring us to battle? If he controls clan Murray's warriors, he could easily field as many warriors as us."

"John's no fool," Quinn replied. "He knows an all-out battle between us and the Murrays would result in heavy losses on both sides. He wants to avoid that. So he's raiding our lands - in all directions to try to force us into acting rashly, before we're ready."

"We should ride out," Fraser said, his hand curling into a fist where it rested on the table top. "Take a force down to Castle Carigg and catch them unawares! If that bastard wants a war, we'll give him one!"

The men nodded in agreement, banging their cups on the table.

Robert held up a hand. "Peace, Fraser. I'm itching to teach the bastard a lesson as much as ye are but everything we've discussed here is just conjecture. Until we know for sure what he's up to, we canna do anything. I'll not risk a feud with the Murrays until we're sure."

Quinn nodded. His brother was a fine warrior but an even finer thinker. He always thought things through before acting - a skill some of the younger hotheads would do well to emulate.

"Matty, Dougal, Callum, ye'll ride out in the morning and take the description of these brigands to all the villages. Tell the aldermen there to be on their guard and to send word to us here at Dunbreggan the minute they spot anything suspicious. The farmers are to bring their animals into the lower pastures and set guards as much as is possible. I'll nae lose more animals to these bastards if it can be helped."

The three men nodded. "Aye, laird. We'll leave at first light," Matty said.

"In the meantime we'll need to send scouts to discover if these rumors about John de Clare and Laird Malcolm's daughter are true."

"I'll go," Quinn said. "I can track them to where I saw the brigands last and pick up their trail from there."

Robert shook his head. "Nae, Quinn, it canna be you. John de Clare knows ye too well. Besides, I need ye here. Ye may be my best warrior but ye are also my heir until the wee one is born. Yer place is here, protecting Dunbreggan."

Quinn nodded reluctantly. He didn't like to be reminded that he was currently the heir to the clan holdings. He'd never wanted the position, just as Robert hadn't. If their eldest brother had lived... Well, he'd learned you didn't always get want you wanted in life.

"I'll go," Fraser said. "I'll get hold of some clan plaid and sneak into their lands. I'll pose as a merchant. It should nae be hard to find goodwives willing to gossip."

"Are ye sure of this?" Robert asked. "It will be dangerous. If ye should be discovered..."

"I'm sure," Fraser replied. The warrior was nothing if not brave.

Robert nodded. "That's settled then. We'll begin preparations in the morning. For tonight, let's enjoy ourselves and celebrate being home."

The men cheered at that.

Darcy listened in silence to the conversations going on around her. Everyone seemed in high spirits, despite the threat Quinn and the others had been discussing earlier. Their laird had returned safely, the hunters had brought down a stag to feed the clan and their lady was soon to give birth to the clan's heir.

That seemed enough. These people demonstrated an uncanny ability to live in the moment.

She picked up her spoon and ate some of the thick stew a servant placed in front of her. It had the gamey taste of venison and was delicious. There was soft white bread to go with it and an earthy ale to wash it down with. Darcy found she was ravenous and soon emptied the bowl, wiping it clean with a piece of bread.

"That's it, my dear," Rebecca said with a smile. "There's plenty more where that came from." She signaled a serving girl over. "Bring Lady Darcy a second bowl would you? It seems she's hungry."

"I am," said Darcy, nodding. "This stew is wonderful. My compliments to the cook."

"I'll be sure to tell Agatha," Rebecca replied. "She'll be mighty happy to have a guest complement her food so."

"You just wait until pudding," Lily said. "Agatha's spicy dumplings are to die for."

Rebecca pulled a face and rubbed her belly. "Not for me. Ever since this little monster came along, I've lost all taste for those dumplings. Roasted chestnuts. Now, I could eat those until I'm sick."

"What a lovely thought!" Lily replied. "And here's me thinking you were a lady!"

"Whatever gave you that idea?" Rebecca replied with a mischievous smile.

Darcy found herself laughing at their banter. She was surprised at how warm and welcoming they both were. They didn't seem at all wary of a stranger amongst them - Quinn had vouched for Darcy and that seemed enough for them.

But their easy acceptance made her worry as well. What would they think when they discovered the truth? That she'd come from the future? Would they believe her? Or would they brand her a liar? Or worse, a witch?

Darcy took a long swig of ale to hide her discomfort. What should she tell them? Something close to the truth but believable. Something that would enable her to get their help whilst she found a way to go home. She hated lying to them but what choice did she have?

Laird Robert finished his meal and pushed his plate away. He leaned back in his chair, laying an arm across his wife's shoulders.

"I hope ye've been looking after our guest well, my love," he said, nodding at Darcy.

Rebecca raised an eyebrow at her husband. "Are ye implying that I'd do anything else?"

"Of course not," Robert laughed. "I'm only teasing ye." He turned to look at Darcy who forced herself to meet his powerful gaze. "So, Lady Darcy. Quinn tells me yer from the Americas. Tell me, how did ye come to be in MacFarlane lands? Did the Spanish bring ye? I've heard rumors they are colonizing the lands over the ocean."

Darcy saw her chance. "I, yes, sort of. I came to Edinburgh for a conference, um, a..." she searched for an appropriate description. "A clan gathering. I went driving, I mean, riding, when I stumbled into the brigands Quinn told you of."

Robert frowned. "Ye went riding in the wilds on yer own? Did ye not ken it isnae safe for a woman to be out without an escort?"

What was she supposed to say to that? These people had very different attitudes towards women's safety. "I didn't realize that," she replied. "In my homeland it's perfectly safe for a woman to go out alone. We do it all the time."

Her tone was a little more challenging than she'd intended.

Robert smiled wryly. "My apologies, my lady. I shouldnae assume such things. This America sounds like an interesting place. Unfortunately Edinburgh is a long way from here and with the raids, it's nae safe for us to take ye there at the moment." He shared a look with Quinn and Fraser. "But ye have my word that as soon as we are able we will escort ye back to yer kin. Until then ye'll be treated as an honored guest here at Dunbreggan."

"Thank you," Darcy said. "Could I ask - how long do you think it will be before it's safe to travel?"

Robert shrugged. "I canna say. A few months maybe."

Darcy started, her breath catching in her throat. A few months? How could she stay here a few months? Her friends would be going crazy with worry! For all Darcy knew, the police were out looking for her right now.

She didn't say any of this though. She smiled her thanks to Laird Robert and tucked into the second bowl of stew that a servant brought her.

There was no way she was going to get stuck here for months. She had to find a way home. No matter what it took.

Chapter 7

Darcy didn't realize she'd been yawning until Rebecca said, "Oh my, that was big enough to swallow me whole!"

Darcy snapped her mouth shut, embarrassed, but Rebecca's eyes were twinkling with merriment. She reached over and laid her hand over Darcy's.

"I'm sorry, here we are gossiping like fish-wives, with nary a thought for how tired ye must be. Ye've been through an ordeal and a half today and that's the truth. No doubt ye'll be wanting some rest."

Darcy smiled sheepishly. "Is it that obvious?"

She was exhausted. She'd been running on adrenaline since her encounter with the brigands but now that adrenaline had run out and she felt like a wrung-out dishcloth. She wanted nothing more than to wrap herself in blankets and shut out the world.

"Alice!" Rebecca called. When the serving girl made her way over, Rebecca said, "Escort Lady Darcy to her room and see she's made comfortable for the night." She turned to Darcy. "Ye need not worry, Darcy. Ye'll be perfectly safe here with us. Things will look better after a night's sleep, ye mark my words."

Darcy nodded and climbed to her feet. Lily rose and gave her a peck on the cheek.

"I'll check in on you tomorrow."

Darcy nodded her thanks and followed Alice towards the door to the great hall. She glanced back as they reached the steps, hoping that Quinn might want to speak to her. He didn't. In fact, he didn't as much as glance in her direction. He was deep in conversation with his brother, the two of them leaning close and talking in hushed voices.

A flash of annoyance went through Darcy. Quinn had insisted on bringing her here and now he ignored her! Well fine, if that's the way he was going to be, she didn't care.

She stomped up the stairs to her room and allowed Alice to help her out of the dress. A white night gown had been left out on the bed which Darcy pulled over her head before climbing into the big four-poster. Alice left a candle burning on the nightstand and then pulled the door closed.

Darcy thought she'd never be able to sleep with what she'd been through today but she was wrong. As soon as her head hit the pillow, she fell into a deep slumber.

She is walking through a misty landscape of heather-clad hills. She can hardly see anything in front of her and the sounds are oddly muffled. "Hello?" Darcy shouts into the mists. "Is anyone there?" Something moves off to her left. A shadow rears up, reaching for her. Darcy screams and scrambles away, running into the mists. But the shadow is in front of her this time. It reaches out, a hand reaching to grab her. "There's nobody to save ye now, lass." It speaks with the voice of the brigand. Darcy turns and runs. The shadow is everywhere now. Everywhere she turns it looms out of the mist. It reaches for her. "Ye are ours now, lass."

Darcy lurched upright with a cry. It took a few terrifying seconds for her to realize she was safe in her room. The shadows in the corners weren't monsters but pieces of furniture. She wiped a hand across her sweat-soaked forehead then threw back the covers and jumped out of bed. Her heart was thumping so fast she could barely think.

Just a dream, she told herself. *Just a dream.*

It didn't help. She crossed to the window and threw open the drapes. It was just getting light and through the window she could see the Highlands stretching into the distance.

She gulped. The enormity of her situation closed in. She was miles and years from where she should be. She must get home. There was no other choice.

Keep calm, she told herself. *Reason it through. Find an explanation. How did you come to be here?*

She thought back to the events of the day. Everything had been going fine until she hit that deer on the road. Then she'd followed it through that stone arch and everything changed.

That's it, she thought. *The arch. That must be the portal. If I can find it again, it will take me home. It's on the shore of the loch so logically all I have to do is follow the line of the shore.*

She closed her eyes, trying to calm her nerves, but images of the shadow creature from her dream formed in her mind, making her heart thump with fear. Pulse racing, she crossed to the wardrobe. She had to go now, before anyone was awake. Fear leant urgency to her steps.

Luckily her own clothes had been stored in the wardrobe. Hurriedly she changed into her jeans, t-shirt and boots. Lastly, she swung her bag over her shoulder, lit the candle and hurried to the door.

The corridor outside was dark and empty. She inched along it and down the steps into the main hall. She froze at the bottom when she realized people were sleeping down here, curled up in their cloaks round the fire. She crept around the edge of the hall, careful to make no sound and reached the door which she pulled open just enough for her to slip through.

Once outside she headed for the causeway. The only people she saw were the guards on the battlements. She waited until their pacing took them away from her and then scurried down the causeway as fast as she could and took a left turn along the shore of the loch, heading south towards where she hoped she'd find the stone archway.

She cast a look over her shoulder as she walked. Dunbreggan rose out of the loch behind her, candles flickering in some of the windows. Was Quinn in one of those rooms? How would he react when he discovered she'd gone? A twinge of guilt twisted her insides. These people had been nothing but kind to her and here she was, leaving without even thanking them.

Running away again, Darcy? she thought. *No!* she answered herself harshly. *I'm not running away. I'm running towards something. I'm running home.*

But as she made her way out into the sleepy countryside, she felt like a coward.

Chapter 8

Quinn had a bad night. He'd tossed and turned, twisting the sheets around himself and falling into fitful slumber only to jerk awake and begin the whole process again. No matter what he tried, he couldn't get his thoughts to settle. Thoughts of the brigands and the danger they posed to his clan. Thoughts of what they would do to counter it. But most of all, thoughts of the dark-haired stranger who'd burst into his life so suddenly yesterday.

He'd so badly wanted to speak to her before she retired last night. Lord help him, he'd wanted to do much more than that and it had taken all his willpower to keep his attention fixed on his brother as he watched from the corner of his eye as she went up to her room.

He'd made an oath that he'd protect the lass, and that meant shielding her from clan gossip as much as any other danger. It was bad enough that he'd ridden in with her without warning yesterday, which sent tongues wagging no doubt, but if he started paying her attention as well, it would no doubt confirm her opinion of highlander men and Quinn was determined to change her mind in that regard.

So he rose early, dunked his head in the bowl of cold water on his washstand, donned his plaid and made his way downstairs for breakfast. As he emerged into the great hall his eyes were already scanning the room for Darcy. She wasn't there.

Well, he couldn't blame the lass for sleeping in. She'd been through quite an ordeal.

He made his way over to the main table, calling greetings to the few people who were up before him and sat in his customary chair next to his brother's. Old Angus, one of the castle's serving staff brought him a bowl of porridge and a mug of ale which he set to heartily.

A short while later Alice entered the great hall. She stood at the bottom of the stairs, scanning the room and chewing her lip. She looked worried. Before Quinn could say anything, she turned around and went back up the stairs.

Quinn shrugged. Women.

But a short time later Alice appeared again, this time with Rebecca in tow. The two women looked around anxiously as if searching for something.

A spike of alarm went through Quinn. Pushing back his chair, he strode over to them.

"Is something wrong?" he asked.

Worry shone in Rebecca's eyes. "It's Darcy. She's gone."

Quinn's stomach flipped over. "Gone? Whatever do ye mean?"

"I mean she's nae in her room. All her things have gone. She must have slipped out in the night or early this morning."

Quinn found himself cursing under his breath and forced himself to stop. His heart was suddenly beating very rapidly. He spun on his heel and strode towards the main door. Rebecca kept pace with him.

"Where do ye reckon she's gone?" she asked. "And at this ungodly hour?"

"She's trying to get home," Quinn replied. "She did seem pretty determined yesterday."

"Home?" Rebecca asked. "Ye mean Edinburgh? It isn't safe for her to travel there alone!"

"I know that," Quinn growled. "Ye know that. It seems Darcy Greenway doesn't know that, despite how many times I've told her!"

He pulled the doors open and took the steps into the courtyard two at a time. Rebecca halted at the top, watching him go with an anxious look on her face.

"Spare me from headstrong lasses!" Quinn growled as he strode towards the stables. "Especially headstrong lasses who dinna have the sense of a bairn!"

Darcy wasn't finding the going as easy as she'd hoped. In the twenty-first century the shores of the loch were riddled with footpaths, many of them made nice and wide for tourists. In this century, there were no tourists of course and what trails they were seemed to be animal trails rather than anything made by human feet.

She found herself struggling through heather-covered terrain. The ground was hummocky and kept threatening to trip her if she wasn't careful where she put her feet. As much as possible she walked on the tiny strip of beach on the loch's edge but more often than not, the shore was steep sided, forcing her inland.

It was just her rotten luck that the day had turned into one of those rare days where the sky was an unbroken arch of blue, the sun a blazing white ball and the wind non-existent. As a result, by midmorning she was sweaty and panting, made worse by the heavy bag she carried over one shoulder.

"Damn it all!" with a grunt of annoyance, she dropped the bag onto the heather and turned around, taking in her surroundings. There was not a soul in sight. On the far side of the loch she saw a thin column of smoke that might indicate a settlement but her only company were the swallows who flitted low over the heather, catching insects.

Dunbreggan was many miles behind her. Darcy wasn't sure how far she'd walked or how far she had to go before she reached the stone archway. When riding with Quinn yesterday she hadn't taken much notice of how long the journey to Dunbreggan had lasted.

She slumped onto a tussock to take a breather. She was hungry and thirsty. In her haste she hadn't even stopped to pack food and drink and as a result she'd eaten nothing since the night before. If she didn't reach the stone archway soon she'd be drinking from the loch and be damned with the consequences.

A noise caught her attention. She went very still, listening. There it was again. The jingle of tack and soft stomp of horses' hooves. Darcy sprang to her feet, looking for a place to hide.

Her only option was a small outcrop of rock several paces ahead. She ran, hunched over to avoid notice, picking up a branch that had washed up on the loch shore. It was a poor weapon but it was better than nothing.

Heart pounding, she ducked behind the outcrop, pressing her back to the damp stone.

Ye belong to us now, lass, said the voice from her dream in her head.

No, she told herself. *It's not the brigands again. It can't be!*

Her pulse was roaring so loudly she could hardly hear anything else. Carefully she peeked out. She stifled a curse as she saw her footprints, so obvious in the wet sand, leading straight towards her.

She waited. Then she heard it. The tell-tale thud of hooves hitting the turf. Her heart fluttered. She dropped her bag to the ground and gripped the branch in both hands. If this was another group of brigands she'd give them a headache they wouldn't forget!

The hooves stopped. For a long time there was silence. Darcy remained stock-still, willing them to move on, to not bother peering behind the outcrop. She crept forward and peeked out.

A horse stood on the other side. It was so close all she could see was its hindquarters and tail that swished at the flies. A man knelt in the sand by the horse. He seemed to be examining her footprints.

Instinct kicked in. There was no way she'd be taken unawares again. She leapt out of her hiding place with a cry, brandishing the branch. The horse shied, throwing up its head and whinnying. Darcy smacked the branch against the man's head with a dull crack.

If she expected him to crumple to the ground she was sadly disappointed. He cursed then spun and grabbed the branch before she could pull it back for another swing. He yanked on the branch and Darcy was pulled forward. She staggered, only just catching herself before she went tumbling to the sand. The man came at her, hands reaching. Darcy ducked under his outstretched arm and aimed a punch at his stomach. He grunted in surprise and Darcy took the opportunity to spin on her heel and start running.

Or she tried, at least.

The man spun as well, his movements quick and sure, and grabbed her arm, pulling her back towards him. Strong hands grabbed her waist and flung her onto her back on the sand. Darcy shrieked in fury and scrabbled to get up but the man threw his weight on top of her, straddling her chest and grabbing her hands which he pinned to either side of her head.

"Ye seem to be making habit of attacking me, lass," said the man. "It's twice in two days I've had to pin ye like this. I'm starting to ken ye don't like me much."

Darcy froze as she recognized the voice. She went limp and looked up into the man's face for the first time.

It was Quinn.

A lump was forming on his forehead from where she'd smacked him. His hair fell forward and lightly brushed Darcy's face. Those blue eyes, so close they dominated her vision, were filled with a stern annoyance.

"I...um...I..." Darcy spluttered.

"Couldn't have put it better myself," Quinn growled.

He stared down at her, his chest heaving from their brief fight. The breath caught in Darcy's throat. He was so close she could feel his breath on her skin. Involuntarily her lips parted.

Quinn leaned down, his own breath quickening, and for the briefest of moments she thought he was going to kiss her. And for the briefest of moments that's what she wanted more than anything else in the world.

But then Quinn blinked. He cleared his throat. "I...um...I..."

"Isn't that my line?" Darcy asked, raising an eyebrow.

He pulled back, releasing her and climbing to his feet. He wiped his brow with the back of his hand then pulled Darcy to her feet.

She stood, a little dazed, trying to figure out what the hell just happened.

"Are ye well?" Quinn asked hoarsely. "Yer not hurt?"

"Only my pride," she replied.

Quinn didn't reply. His expression was stern. "Why did ye run, lass? Were we not hospitable enough for ye? Did we not welcome ye into our household?"

Darcy chewed her lip. "Of course you did. Everyone was lovely. It's just that...it's just..."

Quinn crossed his arms. "Aye?"

Darcy struggled for words. The images from her dream flickered in her memory. She pushed a hand through her hair and slumped onto the sand. "I got scared so I ran," she admitted. "My friend reckons it's what I always do. Perhaps she's right." She looked up at Quinn. "No matter how kind you've all been, I don't belong here. I have to get home."

"So why didnae ye come to me about this?"

"Oh right, like that would have worked. You'd have said, *okay, that's fine. Here's a horse and some provisions. Safe journey.*"

"Nae, I would have stopped you leaving."

Darcy threw up her hands in exasperation. "Exactly! You seem to think you have the right to tell me what I can and can't do! Well I've got news - I don't answer to you!"

Quinn's frown deepened. "I made a vow to keep ye safe, lass! Do ye expect me to just let you go wandering off where you might get yerself killed?"

His tone sounded like the one her father used to use when she'd done something he disapproved of. "That's the point: you don't get to 'let' me do anything, damn it! If I want to go wandering off and get myself killed, that's my own business!"

She wasn't sure that last statement really added to her case but was suddenly furious. With this man who thought he could tell her what to do. With this place that was so alien to everything she knew. With the whole god-damned freaking situation.

"Bah! Ye dinna talk sense, woman! Listen to yer words! Ye sound like a spoiled child throwing a tantrum!" His blue eyes sparked with anger. "I thought I'd helped a sensible, mature, self-reliant woman, not a spoilt child!"

"How dare you? You know nothing about me!"

"Nae," Quinn agreed. "But I was hoping to learn more. Seems yer determined I won't." He bent down to pick up her bag and stomped to his horse where he tied it to the saddle. "Come on. Nae matter what ye say I canna leave ye out here alone. If ye be so determined to get home I'll try to help ye get there."

Darcy, ready for another angry retort, hesitated. "You'll help me? After you've just ridden out here to stop me?"

"Aye."

The anger leaked out of Darcy. This man managed to wrong foot her at every turn. First, he'd ignored her at Dunbreggan as though she was totally unimportant. Then he'd ridden to her rescue only to start ordering her about. Now he was offering to help her. She opened her mouth and shut it again.

"But didn't you say it was close to Murray lands?"

"Aye."

"And isn't it dangerous for any MacFarlane to go there?"

"Aye."

"But you're willing to escort me anyway?"

"Didnae I just say so? I made a vow, lass. I said I'd protect ye and I will, nae matter how much ye rail against it."

Darcy absorbed this in silence. Quinn watched her. He'd gone from angry warrior to patient protector in an instant. She swallowed, her mouth suddenly dry.

"And what would happen to us if we were found on Murray land?"

Quinn shrugged. "Who knows? It depends on whether John de Clare really has taken over the lairdship. If he has it won't end well. He's an evil man who's sworn vengeance on the MacFarlane clan."

Darcy pressed the heels of her hands against her forehead. Her anger became shame. She'd been thinking only of herself, only of how desperately she needed to get back to the archway. Yet Quinn, who'd come after her when he could have easily have left her to her fate, was willing to take her into enemy territory, despite the cost to himself.

Quinn laid a gentle hand on her shoulder. "Are ye all right, lass? I didnae mean to frighten ye. I would never let the Murrays hurt ye, no matter what-"

"It's not that," Darcy said.

She looked up at him. His expression was so sincere. Quinn MacFarlane seemed sincere in everything he did.

"I'm sorry," she said. "I shouldn't have run away. I should have told you what I planned and listened to your advice. It's just that...this is all so confusing."

And you most of all, she thought.

"I understand, lass," he said. "Sometimes we find ourselves in roles and situations which dinna seem right at all but we're in them nonetheless and have to make the best of it." He sounded as though he spoke from experience.

Darcy opened her mouth to ask him about it but he turned away and took the reins of the horse.

"So what will it be, lass? Do ye still wish to travel south? Or will ye consent to return to Dunbreggan with me until we can find a safe way to return ye to yer kinfolk?"

Darcy sighed. "After all the trouble I've caused you still want to take me back? I wouldn't blame you if you left me out here to my fate."

He raised an eyebrow at that. "I canna say I have nae been tempted. Rebecca would have my hide though. She's taken quite a shine to ye."

"Well in that case, I'd better come back with you, hadn't I? It's best not to deny a pregnant woman what she wants unless you want to end up on the wrong side of her temper."

Quinn snorted. "Don't I just know it, lass."

Darcy tipped her head back to look up at him. He watched her, saying nothing. Tentatively, she reached up and gently ran her fingers over the bruise forming on his temple.

"I'm sorry," she murmured. "For hitting you, I mean. I thought you were one of those brigands."

"Forget it," he whispered, his eyes fixed on hers. "I get worse every day in the practice yard."

Quinn's skin felt smooth and warm under her fingertips. She reached up and brushed aside one of the braids that framed his face. Quinn made no move to stop her. He leaned forward and Darcy's eyes slid closed, lips parting slightly, breath quickening.

Quinn cleared his throat and stepped back. "We...um...we'd better get going," he muttered. "Rebecca will be worrying."

"Yes. Of course. Get going. Good idea," Darcy replied, a little flustered.

Quinn held out a hand to help Darcy into the saddle. Darcy ignored his offered help, set her foot in the stirrup and swung easily onto the horse. Did Quinn think she'd never ridden before? She was a vet for pity's sake!

Quinn shook his head in amusement and then swung up behind her, settling his weight and taking the reins. Darcy was trapped between his arms, his warm chest pressed against her back.

Darcy's heart started pounding again, but this time not from fear. Why did Quinn have this effect on her? One minute she was angry with him, the next she was as giddy as a school girl. He was stubborn, bullish and thought he could order her around. But he was also protective, honorable and kind. She didn't know what to make of him.

But one thing was certain. It would be a long ride back to Dunbreggan.

Quinn bit his lip and tried to concentrate on guiding the horse in the right direction. But it was hard. How was he supposed to concentrate with Darcy pressed so close against him? How was he supposed to think straight with her scent all around him, her hair tickling his neck, her warm back pressed against his chest?

He didn't know what to make of Darcy Greenway. She was one of the most insufferable women he'd ever met. Stubborn. Headstrong. Wilful. Disobedient.

Yet she was also strong, intelligent, fiery.

She turned his emotions on their head. When she was around he went from angry to arousal and back again in the blink of an eye. What was he going to do?

He shifted his weight, the saddle creaking beneath him. He hoped she didn't notice how aroused he was with her leaning up against him. That would make this whole situation even worse. His cheeks burned as shame washed through him. What, by all the hells, was he doing?

This woman was lost and alone, without kin or friends. Only a rogue would take advantage of a lass in her position. Today he'd almost kissed her. He'd almost lost himself in those dark eyes of hers. He'd wanted nothing more than to lay her down on the soft turf and make her his.

But he couldn't. He wouldn't. He'd sworn a vow to protect her, no matter how much the damned woman might curse and rail against it. He had a duty and protect her he would, even if that meant protecting her from himself as well.

Nothing could happen between them. He'd see her safe back to her people and that was it.

Darcy found herself drowsing in the saddle.

They topped a rise and Quinn nudged her gently awake. "Darcy? We're home, lass."

She opened her eyes to find them looking down on the loch with Dunbreggan rising from its island in the middle of it. A stab of anxiety went through Darcy. How would the clan react? Would they be angry at her for spurning their hospitality? Would they think her an ungrateful foreigner?

She needn't have worried. Hardly anyone paid them any mind as they rode along the causeway and through the castle gates, perhaps assuming that they'd merely been out riding, and the main hall was fairly empty when they went inside.

Only Rebecca, Lily, and the castle steward were in attendance, sitting with heads together looking at some sheaves of parchment spread out on the main table.

Rebecca looked up when she heard the doors open. A wide smile split her face.

"So ye found our runaway?" she asked, crossing the floor and taking Darcy's hand in hers.

Darcy's cheeks flushed. "I...I'm sorry, Rebecca," she said. "Whatever must you think of me, running away like that?"

Rebecca frowned. "I think yer a young woman who's had a terrible time. One who's found herself amongst strangers and who's desperate to get back to her people. What's wrong with that? I might have done exactly the same in yer position."

She looked at her brother-in-law and her eyes widened as she saw the bruise on his temple. "Yer hurt! Ye didnae run into the brigands again did ye?"

"Nae," Quinn replied, eyes flicking to Darcy, "just had a bit of an argument with a tree branch."

Rebecca looked from Quinn to Darcy and then back again. "Well, I'm glad ye found her and brought her home." Rebecca's clear green eyes fixed on Darcy. "I'm sorry ye felt ye needed to run, Darcy."

Darcy's eyes filled with tears. She'd expected anger from Rebecca and the clan and instead she was getting only kindness and compassion. Her shame doubled. "You've already made me feel welcome, Rebecca. More than I deserve. Can we forget this happened and start again? I'd like it very much if we were friends."

Rebecca waved her hand. "We already are. Any friend of Quinn's is a friend of mine. Here, let's get ye into some proper clothes and let ye get some rest."

"I'd rather be busy, actually," Darcy said. Having nothing to do made her think and thinking made her restless. "Is there something I can do around here? Helping the cook? Helping the servants? I'm not fussy."

Rebecca frowned. "It would nae be seemly for a lady to be doing such work."

Darcy was about to protest that she wasn't a lady but Lily smoothly cut in. "I've got a delivery of cloth coming in today. Why doesn't Darcy come help me sort it? I can give her a tour of the village at the same time."

Darcy smiled at Lily. "I'd love to, thanks."

Quinn cleared his throat. "Right. If ye'll excuse me, I'd better go and see how training is going."

Darcy turned to speak to him as he left but he strode away quickly before she could say anything. She watched with a strange feeling in her stomach as he disappeared out into the sunlight.

"Well, shall we?" Lily asked.

Darcy nodded, gave Rebecca a quick hug, and then followed her new friend outside.

Chapter 9

They crossed the castle grounds and walked together down the causeway to the village on the mainland. It was late afternoon and the sun sparkled on the water. A light wind stirred Darcy's hair and the laughter of a group of children carried on the breeze as they took turns jumping into the loch.

For a moment Darcy could almost forget her worries. It was a peaceful scene.

"You look as though you're a million miles away," Lily said.

"I was just thinking how tranquil it is here. Not like where I'm from. There it's all traffic queues, long days at work, paying bills, vying for promotion. Things seem simpler here."

Lily tilted her head as she looked at Darcy. "I can't say I know of the things you're talking about. This America sounds like a strange place to me. But yes, I understand what you mean. This place, well, it gets into your blood."

"Is that why you didn't return to London?"

"Yes, that and...never mind." She looked away, suddenly blushing.

"Fraser?" Darcy asked. "Rebecca was right wasn't she?"

Lily smiled but it was a sad smile. "It's stupid, isn't it? I keep telling myself I'm wasting my life waiting for him when nothing can come of it."

"Why can't it? If you love each other, what's the problem?"

Lily sighed, staring out over the loch as they reached the end of the causeway. "Fraser has no land, no title. His position comes solely from Laird Robert. Should anything happen to the laird he could find himself with nothing. He's told me countless times he won't take me as a wife only to turn me into a beggar."

Darcy frowned. "That makes no sense. You're a weaver, aren't you? You run your own business. Surely you could support both of you if it ever came to that?"

Lily shook her head. "No man would ever allow his wife to support him. I don't know what America is like, Darcy, but that just simply isn't done here."

Darcy bit back a retort. She had to remember that things were different in this time and she had no right to judge.

"You don't know that," she said. "Maybe you should give him a chance. Don't wait for him to do the asking – you do it. Things only change when somebody is brave enough to do it first."

Lily smiled but didn't answer.

They reached the end of the causeway and entered the village. It was a large settlement with stone-built houses with thatched roofs and a square in the center which housed a well. Lily led her towards the outskirts of the settlement to her weaver's shop. It sat on its own with a small kitchen-garden out the back and a herd of honking geese that hissed at Darcy as she made her way up the path to the rear door.

"Take no notice," Lily said. "They'll not attack you while I'm here."

"And what about if you're not here?" Darcy murmured. "They look like they want to eat me for dinner!"

Lily laughed lightly. "Far better than guard dogs, believe me. Nobody can sneak up on my shop in the night without me knowing."

Inside, the shop was divided up into two large rooms, one where Lily stored her materials, the other where her loom was set up. There was a smaller room at the back that was currently used as a scullery. Upstairs were Lily's sleeping quarters, a modest, whitewashed room set into the eaves of the house.

"This is wonderful," Darcy breathed as she was shown around. "How on earth do you run all this yourself?"

"With difficulty," Lily replied with a laugh. "I keep telling myself I'll take on staff or at least an apprentice but I think I like everything my own way too much. I wouldn't trust anyone else to do things how I wanted them."

Darcy nodded. "I'm with you on that one. I'm a bit of a control freak myself."

There was a knock on the door.

"Excellent," Lily said. "Rolf is here with my shipment! Put the kettle on the stove would you? I think we'll need refreshment to get through this - Rolf can haggle with the best of them!"

The afternoon passed pleasantly. Rolf turned out to be a huge shaggy bear of a man from Holland who traded in the finest Flemish wool. By the way he and Lily haggled good-naturedly it was obvious they'd known each other a long time. Eventually a deal was struck and they all celebrated with a dram of whisky. After Rolf left Darcy spent the time helping Lily catalog and store her wares in the back room.

"You must find this very boring," Lily said as they stowed away a thick bale of wool ready to be spun into plaid for the clan. "You being a lady and everything."

"Lady?" Darcy snorted. "I wish everyone would stop calling me that. I'm not a lady."

"Oh? Then what are you?"

"A veterinarian."

Lily stared at her, baffled.

Darcy thought of how best to explain it. "I'm a healer. For animals."

Lily still looked none the wiser.

"If someone has a sick animal, they can bring it me and I give it medicine," Darcy explained. "For example, if a farmer's cows have colic or a horse has gone lame, I can fix it."

"That sounds like a mighty skill," Lily replied. "I know half the crofters round here would dearly like to have someone they can call on when their animals take sick. Maybe you could do something here in Dunbreggan?"

"I'd love to," Darcy replied, a little spark of hope flaring inside her. That would be just what she needed to keep her busy until she could get home. And it would be a way for her to earn her keep rather than being reliant on Quinn. Being reliant on Quinn MacFarlane was the last thing she wanted. Thoughts of the big warrior brought confusing feelings of annoyance and attraction. She pushed them resolutely away. She would not think of him. She wouldn't.

"But how would I do it?" she pondered aloud. "I'd need somewhere for a clinic." *And there's no way I'm going to ask Quinn's permission to set up at the castle.* She could well imagine his look of disapproval if she did that.

Lily looked around the small room. "Well, how about here? I can easily move this cloth to the other room. It's not much but it's a start."

Darcy clapped her hands together. "Seriously? You wouldn't mind? That would be wonderful!"

"Of course I mean it!" Lily said, laughing. "Seeing as you're staying a while, it might help you keep out of trouble!"

Darcy blushed - Lily was referring to her running away this morning. "Thank you, Lily."

Lily waved her hand. "You're welcome. I know what it's like to be in a strange place where everything is different to what you're used to. The MacFarlanes welcomed me, made me part of the family. It's only right that I should extend that same kindness to you."

Darcy crossed the room and folded Lily into a hug. The other woman laughed lightly and returned the embrace. It felt good to have made a friend. Really good.

Once they'd finished sorting out Lily's stock, the weaver declared it was time for Darcy to be getting back to the castle.

"It will be time for the evening meal soon and Rebecca will worry if you're not there. She takes her charges very seriously."

They shut up Lily's shop and strolled back through the village. All the way Darcy's mind was filled with thoughts and plans for her new veterinary practice. There would certainly be enough patients. Everywhere she looked there were animals - dogs, cats, horses, donkeys, geese, chickens, and of course this didn't include the sheep and cattle that dotted the hillsides roundabout. She was looking forward to it. Until she was able to get back to the stone arch, it would take her mind off things. A bit of normality was what she needed.

Once back in Dunbreggan they took a leisurely stroll around the grounds. Darcy hadn't had the chance to see much of it so, true to her word, Lily gave her a guided tour. She showed her the kitchens, the kennels, the stables - which Darcy inspected with a critical eye and concluded that the horses and dogs were very well cared for - and lastly the practise grounds.

The clan warriors were being put through their paces. Around twenty or so men were stripped to the waist, taking turns to fight with wooden practice swords. The sight had gathered a group of spectators - serving girls for the most part - who giggled behind their hands as they watched the young men spar.

Darcy felt her steps slowing as her eyes fell on Quinn. He was sparring with Fraser, both of them wielding a practice sword as long as their arm. Quinn appeared to be having the upper hand. He beat on Fraser's sword in a flurry of blows that sent the younger man staggering back. Quinn spun, altering his angle of attack and flicked the wooden blade from Fraser's grasp. It went spinning through the air and landed in a puddle.

Quinn frowned down at the younger man. "Ye took yer eyes off me," he said in a stern voice. "Do that in a real battle and yer dead. How many times do I have to tell ye not to let yerself get distracted?"

"I...um...I..." Fraser stammered. His eyes slid to Lily and he blushed. "Sorry, Quinn. It willnae happen again."

Quinn followed the line of Fraser's gaze and saw Darcy and Lily standing there. Darcy began to lift her hand to wave but Quinn's frown deepened and he looked away, calling for his men to form up.

Darcy crossed her arms. Was he deliberately rude or did he just not realize how thoughtless he could be?

But despite her annoyance, Darcy couldn't help but stare as he began putting the men through their paces again. He moved with such deadly grace. He reminded Darcy of a panther - all rippling muscle and easy poise. Although his body was strong and thickly muscled he was as light on his feet as a ballet-dancer, spinning and ducking and pivoting in the blink of an eye.

Lily raised an eyebrow at her. "Ah, I see you've joined the Quinn fan club."

"What do you mean?"

"Don't worry, you're not the first and you certainly won't be the last. Quinn has always been popular with the ladies of the clan. Not one has snagged his heart though. Maybe that's starting to change, eh? He seems quite taken with you."

"Taken with me?" Darcy snorted. "Hardly. He treats me like a naughty school girl most of the time, when he acknowledges me at all. He's like an overbearing elder brother - so serious all the time."

"Can you blame him after what happened to his brother? Quinn's always been the brooding type but he got much worse after Duncan."

Darcy looked at Lily. "What do you mean?"

"He hasn't told you?"

"No. He's not exactly forthcoming with me. What happened to Duncan?"

Lily sighed. "It's a sad tale. Painful for the clan. Most don't like to talk about it but if you're going to be staying here a while it's important you know. As I said, Laird Robert and Quinn had an elder brother, Duncan. He was the laird of the clan and a stronger, fairer laird you couldn't wish for. Quinn and Robert both idolized him. But a few years ago Duncan's party was attacked on the road. Duncan, and the clansmen with him were all killed. Quinn was the only survivor - and he was seriously injured. Robert became laird and Quinn became his heir. I think Quinn blames himself for not being able to save his brother. It's part of the reason Quinn is so protective. He's determined the same won't happen to Robert or anyone else from the clan."

Darcy bit her lip and looked over at Quinn. A wave of shame washed through her. It all made sense now. No wonder Quinn was so wary of brigands on the road. No wonder he was so determined she wouldn't put herself in danger. He'd sworn to protect her, just as he'd sworn to protect his brother. She had deliberately put herself in harm's way, making it difficult for him to keep his oath. What must that have felt like for him? Although she hated to admit it, she owed him an apology.

As Lily took her arm and steered her back towards the castle, she promised herself that she'd seek Quinn out. After all, if she was going to be here a while it made sense be on half decent terms with the laird's brother. That's all it was. Right?

Chapter 10

Darcy hoped to be able to speak to Quinn at dinner. As it turned out though, he didn't come to the high table to sit with his family but instead sequestered himself with his men over at their table by the door. Fraser sat next to him and the two of them spent most of the meal deep in conversation.

Darcy couldn't help but think he was avoiding her.

"What's this I hear about ye setting up shop with Lily?" Rebecca asked her. The laird's wife was wearing a beautiful blue gown, one that Lily had made especially for her pregnancy. The color set off her eyes.

Darcy tore her gaze away from Quinn. "What? Oh, yes. I'm going to start a veterinary practice in Lily's spare room."

Rebecca grinned and shook her head. "Ye know what? I'm nae gonna even ask what that means. Good luck to ye, dear. We could do with more women folk following Lily's lead."

"I thought it was generally frowned upon for women to set up their own businesses," Darcy replied, a little surprised by Rebecca's support.

"Foolish nonsense," Rebecca replied. "We only say that to smooth over male pride. Who de ye think really runs a clan? The laird?" She glanced at her husband who was tucking into his dinner. Rebecca leaned close and whispered conspiratorially. "Hardly. If the men upped and left, this clan would carry on regardless. But if the women did the same? There'd be chaos!" She winked at Darcy. "Besides, yer American aren't ye? We need to make allowances for yer strange ways!"

Darcy laughed. Neither Rebecca nor Robert had mentioned her running away this morning and Darcy was profoundly grateful. She'd been dreading explaining herself to Robert but it appeared Rebecca had done that for her. She hoped she'd be able to repay these people's kindness somehow. Perhaps setting up her veterinary practice would help her do that.

After the meal Darcy returned to her room to change and refresh and then went looking for Quinn. He wasn't in the main hall or on the practice field. After asking around she was directed to the blacksmith's shop.

Darcy approached the building and stopped outside. It was growing dark and candlelight was spilling through the windows. The door to the cottage which stood next to the smithy was open and through it laughter floated out into the dusk.

Darcy halted at the open door. Inside she could see one large room with a fire merrily dancing in the hearth. Quinn was standing by the fireplace, holding a girl of about eight upside down by her ankles. The girl shrieked with mock outrage and three other children of varying ages clustered about Quinn howled with laughter. Quinn put the girl down and she scrambled up, laughing every bit as hard as her siblings.

A large man who Darcy guessed was the blacksmith sat at a well-scrubbed table. "Will ye leave Quinn alone ye little beasts?" the man said. "He canna walk through the door without ye all mobbing him!"

The children took no notice. One of them, a boy of about six, piped in a shrill voice, "Will ye come and see my cat, Quinn? She's having kits she is!"

Quinn leaned down and ruffled the boy's hair. "Aye, of course I'll come and see, William. Just let me have a word with yer da, first."

Quinn seated himself next to the big man who poured them both a dram of whisky. One of the children, a girl little more than a toddler, crawled into Quinn's lap. He wrapped one arm around her as she leaned back against him and went to sleep.

Darcy blinked. She felt like an intruder watching this homely scene. Was that really Quinn in there? Laughing and joking and playing with children like he had not a care in the world?

She had no right to intrude on this private moment. She turned to leave. But the smith's voice suddenly called, "Who's there?"

Darcy froze.

The children came pelting to the door. "It's that new lass!" the elder girl cried. "The one from America!"

Ah. It seemed everyone had heard about her.

Quinn passed the sleeping toddler to her father and came to the door. "Darcy? Is everything all right?"

Darcy found herself blushing. She felt stupid for coming over here. "Yes, of course. Everything's fine. I just-"

"Don't leave the lass standing out in the dark, Quinn!" the smith bellowed. "Bring her in!"

Darcy followed Quinn inside. The children went quiet, staring at this stranger with large eyes.

"Don't stare so, ye little monsters," their father chided them. "Have nae I taught ye better manners than that?"

The smith held out his hand for Darcy to shake. "I'm very pleased to meet ye, my lady. My name's Owen, and I'm the clan blacksmith."

Darcy shook his hand. It was rough and calloused from long days at the forge. "Very pleased to meet you, Owen. And please, call me Darcy."

"As ye say. Now, be seated, please. Quinn was just passing around the whisky again."

Quinn raised an eyebrow at Owen. "Ye are a devil, Owen MacFarlane," he said. "I've told ye I canna set to drinking tonight. I'm on early patrol in the morning."

Owen chuckled. "Aye, I know. Just one more then, to welcome our guest."

Darcy took the cup she was offered and sipped the whisky. It was so hot and fiery she almost choked. The children soon overcame their shyness and began firing a hundred questions at Darcy, so quick she could hardly keep up.

"Where's America?"

"Do they have kittens there?"

"Did ye ride yer horse over the sea?"

"Do ye live in a castle like this one?"

Darcy laughed at the onslaught. "Whoa!" she cried. "One at a time!"

She answered their questions patiently and then shifted along the table to allow the elder girl to set up a stones board which she insisted Darcy play with her.

"Ye've done it now," Quinn said. "Mary will have ye here for hours. Stones is her latest fad."

Mary stuck her tongue out at Quinn. "Ye just don't want to play because I always win!"

"Exactly," Quinn agreed. "Yer too clever for me by far, Mary."

Mary beamed at the compliment.

Darcy followed Mary's instructions and soon got the hang of the game. As they played, Darcy glanced at Quinn. He was sat back in his chair, the toddler on his lap, watching with a smile.

When she'd come to find Quinn tonight, this wasn't what she'd expected. He seemed different. Relaxed. Happy, even. He and Owen bantered back and forth like old friends, Owen's children butting in and demanding Quinn's attention which he gave with a smile and a laugh.

Just as predicted, Mary won the game of stones. The eight year old's obvious delight made Darcy smile.

"Quinn was right, Mary. You're just too smart for me."

"Best of three?" Mary asked hopefully.

Darcy held up her hands in surrender. "Oh, I think I've learned my lesson going up against you."

"Quinn!" William, the six year old whined. "Will ye come and see my cat now? Ye promised!"

Quinn laughed. "All right! I'll come. Here, Owen, take Martha, I dinna want to wake her."

He gave the toddler back to her father and rose. "Right, ye little terror. Where's this cat of yers?"

"This way!" cried William, spinning towards the door. "Will ye come too, Lady Darcy? Will ye?"

"Of course," said Darcy, pushing back her chair.

William grabbed her hand and led her and Quinn round to the smithy. Tucked in the corner of the room was a blanket-filled box. A large orange tabby lay inside.

"Isn't she grand?" William beamed. "I reckon she's gonna have ten kits at least!"

Darcy crouched by the cat. She looked to be a good body weight and her eyes and ears were clean. She purred loudly as William stroked her.

"Ten?" Darcy said. "I'm betting on eleven!"

"Ye reckon? Da! Lady Darcy reckons Tabs will have eleven kits!" William went racing off to tell his father this momentous news.

Darcy straightened. Quinn was leaning against one of the workbenches with his arms crossed, watching her with a small smile on his face.

"It seems ye have a way with children as well as beasts, lass."

"I could say the same for you," Darcy replied. "You were a natural with Owen's children. I never would have believed it."

Quinn shrugged. "I've known them their whole lives. I was apprenticed to Owen for many years. When his wife died I became something of a surrogate older brother to the little uns."

"You're a blacksmith?" she asked, surprised.

"Was," Quinn corrected her. "I dinna have the time to practise these days." He cocked his head at her. "I didnae expect to see ye here tonight. Why did ye come, lass?"

Darcy glanced at him and away again. "I...um...I..." She pulled in a deep breath and schooled herself to calmness. Why did he make her thoughts flutter like this? Dratted man! "I came to apologize."

He lifted an eyebrow and she could swear he looked amused. "Apologize?"

Darcy frowned. Trust him to make this harder for her. She plowed on regardless. "For this morning. I gave no thought to the effect it might have on you, on the clan. Especially after what happened to your brother. I'm sorry, Lily told me. Quinn, why didn't you tell me?"

He was silent for a long time and Darcy began to wonder if she'd overstepped the mark by mentioning his brother. But then he sighed.

"It was three years ago but it still feels like yesterday. Duncan and I were on the road when we were attacked by John de Clare and his men. He wanted revenge on Duncan because he'd exposed him to the king for taking bribes in return for favors at court. Cost de Clare his land and title - almost his life. So de Clare killed Duncan in an ambush. I couldn't save him. Until then I'd never taken my warrior training seriously ye see. I was the youngest of three brothers and my life was destined for the forge. If I had been a better warrior things might have turned out differently. Since then I know I've become a little... what's the word? Stern? Brooding? They're the words Rebecca uses. She's always telling Robert and I to put it behind us. But, Lord, it's hard."

"But not here?" Darcy asked, gesturing at the smithy around them. "You seem so different when you're here. Carefree. Happy."

"Aye, well, I loved being a smith. I loved taking an ordinary piece of metal and creating something wonderful. They say that warriors earn all the glory. I disagree. It's the craftsmen that deserve our songs. They're the ones who create beauty."

"But now you're the leader of the clan's warriors and heir to the lairdship. And you never wanted either position?"

From the tightening of his jaw Darcy knew she'd guessed right. His hand, resting lightly on his thigh, curled into a fist. "Aye. Something like that. I have a duty. To protect my people. My clan. I willnae let what happened to Duncan happen to anyone else."

Darcy didn't reply. She found herself staring at him. This man was such a tangled up ball of emotions. She didn't know what to make of him.

Quinn pushed off the bench. "I've got something for ye, lass. Follow me."

He led Darcy to the back of the shop. A wrapped bundle was sitting on the bench surrounded by tools. Quinn picked up the bundle and held it out to Darcy.

"For me?" Darcy asked, taking the package. It was heavier than she expected. "What is it?"

"Something to keep ye safe," Quinn said. "Especially if yer gonna insist on more escapades like this morning."

Ignoring his jibe, she unwrapped the bundle to reveal a long dagger. The handle had been carved into the semblance of a wolf. It was beautiful.

"You made this?" she asked.

"Aye," Quinn replied. "I've been working on it for a while, not sure who I would give it to. Seems I was making it for ye without knowing it. Do ye like it? I can change the handle it you dinna-"

"It's perfect," Darcy breathed. "Beautiful."

She ran her hand over the handle, feeling the detail of the running wolf. It was exquisite. No wonder Quinn missed working the forge when he had skills like this.

"I thought the handle did suit ye," Quinn said. "As brave and fierce as one of the noble creatures. A little she-wolf."

Darcy looked up to find he'd stepped closer and was looking down at her, his eyes deep and mesmerizing. Longing flashed through Darcy.

"Quinn, I-"

He cupped her face in one hand and kissed her.

Darcy's eyes slid closed. She melted into his embrace as his arms encircled her. His kiss deepened, growing hungry. Darcy's thoughts scattered as desire raced along her nerves.

Then he suddenly broke away, stepping back and leaving Darcy dazed and breathless. He shook his head as if to clear it.

"Darcy, I'm sorry," he murmured. "I shouldnae have done that. I don't know what came over me."

The mask was coming down again. The stern warrior replacing the carefree blacksmith.

"Don't I get a say in this?" Darcy said, exasperated. "You think I'd let you kiss me if I didn't want it?"

He frowned. "Ye don't know what yer saying. Yer confused, a long way from home and I have duties. I'm bound to my clan, while yer-"

"An outsider?" she finished for him angrily.

"That's not what I meant, lass." He scrubbed a hand through his hair and blew out his cheeks. "Look, let me escort ye back to yer room."

"Don't worry," Darcy snapped. "I can find my own way back."

She spun on her heel and stomped out of the smithy. All the way back to the castle she seethed with a mixture of hurt and anger. She was angry with Quinn for blowing hot and cold but most of all she was angry with herself. She was angry she'd started letting down her defenses. Insufferable man! Who the hell did he think he was playing with her emotions like this?

She clutched the dagger to her chest. A gift. Why had he given it to her? Did he even realize how confusing he was? Darcy pressed her mouth into a tight, flat line and made a promise to herself. No more of this. It would be better for everyone if she kept out of Quinn MacFarlane's way.

Quinn watched Darcy disappear into the night. He wrapped his arms around himself as if cold. He longed to run after her, take her into his arms and kiss her into submission.

Which is exactly why he didn't move.

He couldn't go down this road. Darcy turned his world on its head. When she was around he couldn't think straight. One minute he was annoyed, the next he was breathless with longing. She filled his thoughts every minute and turned his emotions into a tangled knot. He couldn't allow it. Now, more than ever, he had to be focused, clear-headed. The clan was in real danger from de Clare and his men and it was Quinn's duty to keep them safe.

And besides, Darcy had made it clear she would be going home the second she got the chance. Where would that leave Quinn?

No, he thought. *I have to stay away from her. Being close is too dangerous.*

Dougal was taking a long range scouting trip out tomorrow morning. They'd be gone for days at least, maybe weeks. Perfect. Quinn would volunteer to join them. Some time away was exactly what he needed. Maybe that would help him forget Darcy Greenway.

Chapter 11

"What are ye thinking of?" Rebecca asked. "Ye look like yer miles away."

Darcy startled and pulled her gaze away from the window. Gray rain sheeted down outside, obscuring the castle grounds and everything else within more than a few feet. It had been this way for days.

"Oh, nothing," Darcy lied. In truth, she was thinking of *him* again. It seemed that staring at the rain and thinking about Quinn took up most of her time recently.

She'd not seen him since the incident at the forge, over a week ago.

She missed him. Oh, she'd never admit that to him of course, pig-headed idiot that he was.

"Come on then. Try again."

Darcy sighed. "I'm never going to get the hang of this."

"Oh, ye will!" Rebecca said in a stern voice. "Ye just have to keep practicing."

Darcy pursed her lips, concentrating on the words in front of her and then carefully read the Gaelic sentence aloud, pronouncing each word slowly and deliberately.

Rebecca grinned. "Ye don't want to know what ye just said. I'm not sure it's polite to repeat it in civilized company!"

"See?" Darcy snapped the book shut with a thump. "I'll never get the hang of Gaelic."

"I don't believe it's really the difficulties of our language that have ye on edge this morning, my friend. Am I right? Is it not the presence, or lack thereof, of one certain dark-haired brute?"

God, was she that obvious?

"Of course not," she said indignantly. "Quinn's an idiot!"

"Ye'll get no argument from me there! But tell me, what's he done to ye for ye to arrive at the same conclusion?"

Rebecca's face was all innocent curiosity. For a moment Darcy longed to tell her everything. About the amazing kiss she and Quinn had shared. About the way her skin turned to flame when his lips touched hers. About the way her stomach twisted when he was near.

And about the way Quinn had rejected her.

That hurt more than anything and Darcy was annoyed with herself for feeling that way. After all, she was going home wasn't she? As soon as she found a way to find the stone arch again, she'd be gone. So why was she hurt by the way Quinn had reacted? And if he really felt nothing for her then why did he give her that dagger?

It was all very confusing.

Rebecca was watching her expectantly, head cocked to one side.

"Nothing," she mumbled. "It's nothing."

Rebecca sighed but didn't push the issue. She shifted uncomfortably, placing one hand on her swollen belly. A spasm of pain passed over her face.

"Are you all right?" Darcy said, laying a hand on her friends arm.

"I'm fine," Rebecca replied. "It's this little devil. He seems to find it highly amusing to kick his mother whenever he gets the chance."

Darcy laughed. "What have the midwives said?"

"Any day now," Rebecca replied. "And it can't come soon enough!"

Darcy patted her friend's arm comfortingly. She looked around the room. They were in the castle's library, up in the east corner. It was a square room hung with heavy drapes at the windows. Shelves lined the walls packed to bursting with books and scrolls and documents of all kinds. The clan's history and genealogies were kept up here, along with the accounts and records, for which Rebecca as the laird's wife was responsible. Rebecca had offered to begin teaching Darcy Gaelic and Darcy had jumped at the chance. Anything to keep her busy.

Darcy's eyes fell on a stack of rolled-up parchments sitting on a shelf.

"What are those?"

"Maps," Rebecca replied, still stroking her belly. "Of our holdings, our neighbors holdings, and just about anywhere else Robert could get his hands on. He's got a thing about maps."

"Can I see them?" Darcy asked, feeling a stab of excitement.

Rebecca waved a hand. "Be my guest but they're not very interesting."

Darcy crossed over to the bookshelf. She pulled one of the maps down and unrolled it on the big table under the window. It showed a faded line drawing of the MacFarlane estate. Dunbreggan sat in the middle and the land roundabout was divided by lines which indicated each crofter's parcel of land and was labeled with names indicating who worked it.

Darcy leaned forward, biting her lip as she concentrated, scanning the map. The loch was clearly marked and she ran her finger along the shoreline, hoping to find the stone arch labeled somewhere. It wasn't.

Rebecca heaved herself out of her chair and waddled over. "What are ye looking for?"

A magic arch that will take me back to the twenty-first century, Darcy thought. But aloud she said, "Nothing in particular. I'm just interested in the geography around here."

"So ye'll have more success running away next time?" Rebecca said the words with a laugh but Darcy's stomach flipped over.

Was she planning to run again? She didn't have any answers. Her thoughts and emotions whirled in crazy confusion. She was a fish out of water here. These people's ways were so different to anything she was used to.

And yet... and yet... she liked it here. The MacFarlanes had accepted her unquestioningly, both Rebecca and Lily becoming firm friends.

And then there was Quinn. Ah, Quinn.

She shook herself. These thoughts were stupid. He'd made it clear nothing would happen between them. No, Darcy had to get home. She had to. Her patients needed her. Her friends needed her. Gretchen was probably frantic with worry. For all she knew, the police were searching for her right now.

She couldn't let this place seduce her, no matter how much she wanted it to.

The answer might lie in these maps. The stone arch must be marked somewhere.

She smiled at Rebecca, feeling awful for lying to her friend. "Of course not. I'll wait here like a good little woman until Quinn says it's safe."

Rebecca snorted. "A good little woman? I've seen that look in yer eye before. I hope Quinn knows what he's letting himself in for!"

He's letting himself in for nothing, Darcy told herself. *He's made it clear how he feels.* But she smiled along with her friend and then steered the conversation to safer topics.

"Nobody's going to come, are they?" Darcy said despondently.

Lily looked up from her loom. "Give it time. I'm sure they'll come once word gets around."

Darcy nodded but her friend's words didn't make her feel any better. She glanced around the little room at the back of Lily's shop. She'd managed to purloin a large table from Rebecca which she'd scrubbed clean and placed in the middle of the room to act as her examination table. Her bag, which contained her twenty-first century supplies, she'd placed in a locked cabinet in the corner of the room. The bag held equipment and medicines that would give her away instantly should someone discover it so she'd been very careful not to let anyone see the bag's contents. She wasn't sure what she'd do once her limited supplies ran out but she'd cross that bridge when she came to it.

Besides, if this morning was anything to go by, that wouldn't be a problem. It was her first clinic and so far there'd been not a single customer.

She should have known this was a bad idea. What had she been thinking?

Lily sat back and sighed. "You have to have patience," she said. "Do you reckon there were customers flocking at my door when I first set up my shop? It took time. Time for my reputation to spread. Time for people to trust me. They'll come. You'll see."

Sudden shame washed through Darcy. Here she was moping and feeling utterly sorry for herself and not giving a thought to anyone else. Although Lily put on a brave face, Darcy couldn't fail to notice the worry that crossed her face when she thought nobody was looking. Fraser had left a few days ago to infiltrate the Murray clan. It was a dangerous mission and the whole MacFarlane clan was on tenterhooks, Lily more than any of them.

Darcy crossed to her friend and gave her a quick hug. "I'm sorry. You're right, of course. How about I make us some mint tea?"

Lily smiled then stretched her arms over her head, working out the kink in her shoulders. "That sounds lovely."

Darcy filled the kettle and put it on the stove.

A hesitant knock sounded on the door and Owen, the blacksmith poked his head through.

"Hello, Owen," said Lily. "What brings you here? After some new trews? I've just the material to match your eyes!"

"Nae, lass," Owen replied. "I'm here to see Lady Darcy, actually."

"Let me through, Da!" came a young boy's voice.

The door burst open and William came bustling into the room.

"Darcy!" he piped, running over to her. "She's had them! Ten, just like I said! Will ye come see? Ye promised!"

"Whoa! Slow down!" Darcy laughed. She crouched down level with William. "Am I to understand your cat's had her kittens?"

"Aye! This morning. Will ye come see?"

"I'm sorry, Lady Darcy," Owen rumbled. "But he wouldnae stop pestering me until I promised to bring him to find ye. I've not got a stick of work done all morning."

"It's fine, Owen," Darcy said, rising. "I did make a promise after all." She looked down at William and held out her hand. "Well? What are we waiting for? Shall we go and see these kittens of yours?"

William squealed in delight, grabbed her hand and pulled her to the door. Darcy gave Lily one last wave and then allowed William to lead her through the village to his house, a bemused Owen following behind.

Sure enough, the orange tabby had given birth to ten kittens. She was curled around them in a bed of straw in the forge, busily licking them. William crouched beside them and began scratching the momma cat's ears.

"She's a good girl," he said, sounding like a proud grandparent. "She's caring for them real good."

"She certainly is," Darcy agreed. "Would she mind if I checked the kittens? To make sure they're healthy?"

"Nae, Tabs won't mind. Will ye, girl?"

Darcy picked up the kittens one by one, checking their eyes, their ears and sexing each one. "There are seven boys and three girls," she told William, "and they all look as healthy as can be."

William beamed up at his dad who stood at the door watching his son with a bemused smile.

"Ye must look after them, William," he rumbled. "It will take a lot of work to see them all through to adulthood."

William put on an offended expression. "Of course I'll look after them! Can they come in the house, da? Can they?"

"Nae, lad. They'll be fine here."

William pouted, crossing his arms, and Darcy had to laugh at the expression on his face.

"Your da's right, William. This is Tab's den. She'll feel safer here than in the house. I'll come check on them soon and make sure everything's okay. Meanwhile, you need to start thinking of some names."

William picked up one of the little females and held it up. "Well I've already thought of one. This is Darcy!"

"I'm flattered!" Darcy laughed.

With promises to visit again soon Darcy left the blacksmith's household and returned to Lily's shop. William's boyish enthusiasm was infectious and Darcy found that her mood had improved no end by the time she pushed open the door to Lily's shop.

But it took a nose-dive when she saw who was waiting for her in the clinic.

Quinn looked up as she entered the room.

Her heart thudded at the sight of him. She wasn't sure if it was excitement or dread. Maybe a bit of both. She was relieved to see him, of course. Relieved to see him whole and well after all the time she'd spent worrying about him. But as always when he was around, her feelings were suddenly mixed up and confused.

"Darcy," he said in greeting.

"Quinn," she replied stiffly.

He rubbed his chin. "Um...are ye well?"

"Fine. Thank you for asking. When did you get back?"

He winced at her cold tone. "Late last night. I hoped to catch Fraser before he left on his mission to the Murrays but it seems I missed him." Gesturing at the room, he asked, "Rebecca told me I could find ye here. She said ye'd set up a 'clinic'. What's this all about?"

Darcy shrugged nonchalantly. "I told you I'm a vet. Lily was kind enough to help me set up a clinic here. After all, if I'm going to be here a while I'll need to pay my why. I can't rely on charity forever."

"Why?" he asked, a frown marring his face. "Did I not say ye were under my protection? If ye need aught, ye just come and ask me."

"Ask you?" Darcy asked incredulously. "And how exactly could I do that? You've been gone for ages! You left me on my own here!"

"Ye weren't on yer own. Ye had Rebecca to look after ye."

"Rebecca is my friend, not my nursemaid. And I don't need anyone to look after me!"

"Is that so?" Quinn replied. "I've only been away a week and ye've already gone and done something hair-brained. What were ye thinking, lass? It's not right for a lady to being doing something like this. Ye should have come to me afore you set up this venture."

"Why? So you could tell me I wasn't allowed to do it?"

"Aye, and save ye some embarrassment."

Darcy's mouth dropped open. "Save *you* embarrassment you mean!" she yelled. "After all, aren't I 'your responsibility' as you keep reminding me? You don't want tongues wagging about Quinn's odd foreigner and her strange ways do you? We couldn't possibly have anything that might tarnish the mighty Quinn's image!" She'd taken a step towards him and now she faced him with her hands balled into fists. If the table hadn't been between them she might have swung for him.

"Yer my guest, woman!" he growled. "Is it too much to ask that ye do as I say? God above, why couldn't I have found an obedient woman on the road?"

That did it. A cold rage settled in the pit of Darcy's stomach. Obedient? Who the hell did he think he was? He disappeared for weeks and then turned up here telling her what to do!

"This is my clinic," she said. "I'd thank you to get the hell out."

He didn't move. His blue eyes were fixed on hers, assessing. Darcy was well aware that he was the laird's brother and technically all this land belonged to him. If he wanted, he could toss Darcy out on her ear and march her bodily back to the castle.

The silence stretched between them. Then Quinn marched to the door and yanked it open. He paused and looked over his shoulder.

"I'll be riding out again this afternoon, scouting our eastern border. I might be gone a while."

Darcy crossed her arms. "I'll try not to get into too much trouble whilst you're not here to supervise me."

He left without a word, slamming the door behind him.

With a cry of exasperation, Darcy slapped her palm against the table. Insufferable man! He swanned in like he owned the place, making her feel like a naughty schoolgirl, then calmly announced he was leaving again! Darcy pinched the bridge of her nose, fighting back the angry tears that were gathering. She looked around at the little clinic. The empty clinic.

Was Quinn right? Was this an idiotic idea? Would nobody come?

Her heart sank. Quinn, one of the most important people in the clan, didn't approve of her venture. Once word of that got around, her chances of getting any customers were precisely nil.

She balled her hand into a fist again. Damn the man!

Insufferable woman!

Quinn stomped through the village, sending squawking chickens scattering from his path. He knew he was scowling fit to curdle milk but couldn't seem to help it. Far from easing the tension between him and Darcy, his visit had only made it worse. Why did she have to be so difficult? Why couldn't she just do as she was bid like any other good clan woman would?

He paused, glancing back at Lily's shop. In the time he'd been away from Dunbreggan Darcy had filled his thoughts. He'd missed her terribly.

So why couldn't he tell her that? Why had he shied away when they'd kissed last week? Why had he avoided her ever since like a frightened boy? And why was he so annoyed that when he'd returned he'd found that, instead of pining for his return, she'd taken it on herself to set herself up in business, striking out on her own rather than waiting for him to come back and provide for her?

"Quinn, yer a fool, with yer stupid pride," he said to himself.

Darcy's strength, her fire, were why he found her so damned attractive. She kept him on his toes, made him work to please her. He shouldn't be surprised that she'd been busy while he'd been away.

"Ho! Quinn!" called a voice from up ahead.

Old Mac was walking towards him, his dog, Shep, by his side. The old farmer held most of the crofts close to Dunbreggan and he and his family had successfully farmed them for years. He walked with the aid of a staff now but to Quinn's eyes he still seemed as gnarly and strong as an oak tree.

"Mac!" Quinn greeted the old man, slapping his shoulder. "How are ye, ye old bastard?"

"Better now ye and yer men have returned, I'll tell ye. Did ye find anything in yer scouting?"

Quinn winced. He and his men had spent the last week living in the wilds, chasing rumors of brigands and worse in the east of

MacFarlane lands. They'd not found any brigands, only burned out crofts and slaughtered animals. So far, there'd been no human casualties but if this carried on, it was only a matter of time.

"Word has it it's that bastard de Clare," Mac said, his bluff face folding into a scowl. "Is it true he's married Murray's daughter? Bad news for us if he has."

"We've no proof," Quinn replied. "Only rumor. Until we know for definite we can't assume anything."

Fraser had been gone for two days now and there'd been no word. Quinn was worried about the lad. He could hold his own in a fight but wouldn't stand a chance against the might of the Murray clan. Had he done the right thing in sending the lad into danger? He'd never forgive himself if something happened to him.

Quinn's eyes fell on Shep. The old sheepdog was limping, holding up his left paw. "What's yer hound done, Mac?"

"The daft animal still thinks he's a pup, doesn't he? Tried chasing down a hare and came off worst. He's not walked right for days."

"Ye should take him to see Darcy," Quinn said. "She's a vet, ye ken?"

Mac stared at him. Quinn laughed.

"Nae, I'd never heard the word either. But it means she might be able to fix yer hound for ye. She's set up in the back of the weaver's shop."

Mac ran his fingers through his beard. "I'd heard tell of the lass doing some such thing. What do ye make of it?"

Quinn pulled in a deep breath. Old Mac was looking to him for guidance. "She has my patronage," he found himself saying. "And my permission. Pass the word, will ye? Encourage people to go see her."

"Aye, I can do that." Mac looked down at his dog. "Well, come on, ye daft hound. Let's take ye to see this 'vet'."

As the old man walked away Quinn called, "Oh, and Mac? Don't let her know I sent ye? She'll likely wring my neck."

Mac chuckled. "Aye, I understand the way of it, lad. I've been smitten with a lass or two in my time, ye ken. I'll keep my mouth shut."

Quinn watched Old Mac head off. Was he that obvious? Did everyone in the clan know how he felt about Darcy?

Everyone except for Darcy, it seems, he thought. *And it's best if it stays that way.*

Chapter 12

"What do ye reckon then, Lady Darcy?" Angus MacFarlane said, anxiety in his voice.

His wife, Elsa, watched from the doorway, their two-year old daughter Maisie clutched in her arms.

Darcy well understood the crofter's concern. Daisy, the long-haired highland cow who lay in the straw in front of her was Angus and Elsa's main source of income. They made her milk into cheese to supply Dunbreggan. Without her, they'd be in trouble.

"It's nothing serious," Darcy replied. "She has a chest infection. I'll give her some medicine and she'll be fine in a few days."

Angus blew out his cheeks and Elsa sighed in relief. Darcy turned her back on them and rummaged in her bag. Being careful to keep her equipment out of sight she filled a syringe with antibiotic and quickly injected Daisy.

"There," she said, turning to the crofters. "All done. Keep an eye on her the next few days. Come and get me if she takes a turn for the worse."

"We will," Angus said, taking Darcy's hands in his own. "We canna thank ye enough. What can we give ye in return for yer help?"

"Nothing," Darcy replied. "You've all offered me so much kindness and hospitality, this is the least I can do to repay it."

Angus beamed. "Ye are a marvel, Lady Darcy. Quinn is a lucky one to have found ye."

Elsa squeaked and shot her husband a look. "Ignore him, my lady. He never knows when to keep his opinions to himself."

Darcy felt herself blushing. Dear god, did everyone in the clan think she and Quinn were an item? If they only knew the truth! Almost two months had passed since their altercation in Lily's shop. During that time they seemed to have reached an uneasy truce. That basically meant they ignored each other. Oh, they chatted politely enough when they happened to cross paths, but for the most part they avoided each other. That suited Darcy just fine.

That ache in her heart every time she saw him was just annoyance at his behavior. Nothing else. Definitely not.

She closed her medical bag and climbed to her feet. Since that first day her practice had gotten busier and busier. Now she was run off her feet most days visiting the outlying crofts to see horses with bad teeth, sheep with coughs, dogs with limps and a hundred other things besides. Her supplies were already starting to run low. What would she do when they ran out? She had no way of restocking her drugs and medicines. Could she find some kind of local equivalent? She thought she might be able to replicate penicillin if she could get the right equipment.

She shook her head. What was she thinking? It was a moot point. She'd be going home soon. And then it wouldn't matter at all.

Giving Elsa and Maisie a quick hug, Darcy stepped out into the rain. It hadn't let up all day. In fact, it hadn't let up for days on end now. She held her bag over her head as she gingerly made her way to the path that led back down to the village.

What she wouldn't give for a decent raincoat and umbrella!

A figure was running up the path towards her. As it got closer, Darcy realized it was William, the blacksmith's son.

"Lady Darcy!" he cried, skidding to a stop and panting. "Quinn sent me to find ye."

"What is it?" Darcy asked, feeling a spike of alarm.

"It's Old Mac's sheep. They've been trapped by a flood! Quinn and some others have gone to help rescue them! He's asked if ye'll come and help in case some of them are injured!"

"Of course I'll come!" Darcy replied. "Lead the way!"

William took off at a run and Darcy ran after, doing her best to keep up with him in her long gown. The path had turned treacherous and slippery and more than once Darcy stumbled to her knees before hauling herself up and pushing herself on. It took around half an hour before they reached the valley that housed Old Mac's farm.

Darcy skidded to a halt at the sight that greeted her. The valley was flooded. The waters of the stream had risen so far that it had burst its banks, turning the valley bottom into a lake. A group of sheep huddled on a strip of quickly shrinking dry ground on the far side, trapped between the water and a sheer cliff behind them. Darcy could hear the plaintive bleating over the drumming of the rain.

Old Mac and his three sons were down at the bottom along with at least half a dozen men from Dunbreggan. Darcy's eyes sought out Quinn and she found him on the water's edge, shouting orders to the others. He'd stripped to the waist and had a rope tied around his waist, the end held in the anxious hands of the other men. Even as Darcy watched he took a step into the rushing water.

Terror flashed through Darcy. He was going to ford the river! Was he insane? One wrong move, one slip, and he'd be washed away in an instant.

She was running before she even realized it. "Quinn!"

She pelted down the valley side, slipping and sliding in the mud until she reached the bank.

"Ye came," Quinn said.

"Of course I came," Darcy snapped. "What did you think I'd do? Go home and sit by the fire while you're out here?"

A faint smile quirked Quinn's lips. "I suppose not. I'd be grateful if ye would check the animals as we bring them over. Some may be hurt."

Darcy nodded. "Of course." She looked at the raging river and the sheep huddled on the other side. She swallowed. "You're not seriously going to cross that are you?"

"What choice is there? I canna let Old Mac lose half his flock."

Darcy let out a long breath. "Okay. But Quinn, please, be careful."

His eyes met hers. The driving rain, the wind and the cold seemed to recede. "I will, lass. I promise."

He began inching out into the river. In only moments it was up to his knees, then his hips, then his chest. Darcy ground her teeth and clutched her bag so tight her knuckles went white.

William pressed himself into her side, grabbing her skirt. "He's awful brave isn't he?" he said.

"Yes," Darcy said. "Yes he is."

It seemed to take Quinn an age to cross. In reality Darcy supposed it was little more than a few minutes, but for her it was measured in the rapid beating of her heart. Several times Quinn stopped, checked his footing and adapted his route. Twice he stumbled, going under the water to the shocked gasps of those watching on the bank. But each time he emerged unscathed, water streaming off his body and gave them a wave to show he was okay.

Finally he reached the far bank and tied his end of the rope securely around a tree.

Darcy breathed out a sigh of relief. She ran a shaking hand over her brow and then gently peeled William from her side. Crouching down until she was on eye-level with him, she said, "I'm going to need your help now, William. Do you think you could run back to the house and bring as many dry blankets as you can find?"

William nodded, and, eager to have something to do, pelted back up the path towards Old Mac's cottage.

The men on the bank began filing into the river. Each one had a length of rope tied around their waist which in turn was tied to Quinn's anchor line with a clever knot that allowed it to move along the rope already strung across the river.

Old Mac himself went all the way across, joining Quinn on the far bank to catch the sheep. The other five took positions in the river so they formed a human chain.

Darcy positioned herself on the near bank where the rope was anchored to a tree on this side, rolled up her sleeves, tucked the hem of her dress into the tops of her boots and quickly twisted her hair into a knot and tied it with a leather band. She'd need to be able to move freely for the task ahead.

Over on the other side, Old Mac and Quinn grasped the first ewe. The terrified animal bleated pitifully and struggled as the men grabbed her. Quinn hugged her to his chest, catching her legs in one strong arm so she couldn't kick and carried her to the water's edge. He passed her down to the first man who took the struggling beast and handed her to the next man. In this way they carried the sheep along the human line until she reached the far shore.

By the time she reached Darcy the ewe was soaked and terrified and it took all of Darcy's strength, aided by one of Old Mac's men, to manhandle the beast onto the shore. William came pelting back down the trail, skidding and slipping, and dumped an armload of blankets next to Darcy.

"Well done, William," Darcy said, shooting the frightened lad a reassuring smile.

Old Mac's man held the ewe in a firm grip whilst Darcy examined her. First her head, then her teeth, eyes and ears. Lastly she ran a hand along her limbs, checking for breaks or abrasions.

Satisfied, she nodded. "She's fine. Let her go."

Old Mac's man stepped back, releasing the ewe. She scrambled over to the rest of the flock who were huddled under an oak tree halfway up the valley and well away from the rising water.

Already the second ewe was being hauled across the river. As she was pulled up on the bank Darcy bent to her task. Her training took over. She no longer saw the rain, no longer felt the wind or the cold. She didn't even see the men who struggled in the river. All her concentration was focused on the animal in front of her. Time wore on. Luckily most of them were uninjured and were sent up to join the flock at the side of the valley.

"Lady Darcy," William said suddenly. "I think Quinn may be wanting ye."

Darcy looked up to see Old Mac carrying the last ewe down to the river bank. Quinn walked anxiously by his side and he was waving at Darcy and then pointing at the sheep. Darcy couldn't hear his words over the roar of the river but she understood the signal well enough. Something was wrong.

She nodded, surreptitiously checking her bag to ensure she had everything she might need. The men waded out of the river and gratefully grabbed the blankets William had brought, wrapping them around their shoulders and stamping their feet to get warm. Old Mac himself carried the last ewe over. Quinn waited until the old man was safely ashore before untying the rope and wading across. The two men reached the shore and Darcy leaned down quickly as they held the ewe to examine.

It became clear immediately what the problem was. A jagged branch had impaled her, piercing her neck.

Darcy went to her knees by the ewe's side and gently examined the wound. "She's going to need surgery," Darcy muttered. "Get her into the house, quickly."

Quinn carried the injured ewe up to Old Mac's cottage. Darcy ordered everyone but Quinn to wait outside and then scrubbed down the kitchen table before scrubbing her hands and forearms with antiseptic soap.

She took a deep breath. The ewe wouldn't survive unless Darcy could remove the wood, clean and repair any damage and then close the wound. She couldn't do it alone.

She was going to need Quinn's help.

She opened her bag and took out a bottle of sedative and a needle. "Hold her still," she instructed Quinn.

Quinn nodded, doing as she asked.

Darcy quickly injected the struggling ewe then pressed her fingers against the ewe's neck, measuring her heartbeat as she sank into sleep.

"We don't have much time," Darcy said. "I daren't give her too much anesthetic. You're going to have to help me. Don't ask any questions and do exactly as I say. Can you do that?"

Quinn looked at her then at the sleeping ewe. "Aye, I can do that."

"Good." She dug into her bag and laid out the instruments she'd need in a line on the bench.

Quinn's eyes widened at the equipment she revealed but true to his word, he asked no questions.

"Wash your hands," Darcy instructed. "There's antiseptic soap over there,"

Whilst Quinn did this, Darcy examined the sheep. She listened to the chest and was relieved to hear a normal breathing pattern. This meant the branch hadn't pierced the lung or trachea. The biggest threat was blood loss when she removed the branch.

"Are you ready?" she asked Quinn.

He came to stand by her side. "Ready."

"Okay. Pass me those scissors."

Together they set to work. Darcy worked as quickly as possible. Quinn passed her instruments, took away ones she'd finished with and held things in place for her while she worked.

Darcy managed to remove the branch, stitch together the damaged muscle underneath, flush out the wound with antiseptic and then stitch up the wound. Lastly, she gave the ewe a shot of antibiotic and then brought her round from the anaesthetic.

Darcy quickly packed away her equipment and called Old Mac into the room. Quinn lifted the groggy ewe down from the table and handed her to Old Mac.

"She should be fine," Darcy said. "But keep her confined for at least a week until I've taken the stitches out."

Old Mac looked to the ewe, to Quinn and then to Darcy. "I canna believe it," he breathed. "I thought this beast was a gonna for sure. Ye surely are a wonder, Lady Darcy."

She shrugged. "I couldn't have done it without Quinn." She smiled at him. "You've missed your calling in life," Darcy said. "You should have been a shepherd."

"Do ye think so?" Quinn replied with a mischievous smile. He looked at Old Mac. "Do ye need an apprentice, Mac? Darcy thinks I'd make a fine one."

Old Mac snorted. "No disrespect my friend but I think yer too used to the soft life within a castle. I couldnae see ye spending days out on the moors with nowt but yer loyal dog for company."

"Aye," Quinn laughed. "Perhaps there's some perks in being the laird's brother after all."

"I'd say," Old Mac replied. "If ye hadn't been out patrolling ye'd have never found Lady Darcy, would ye? And then where would we be? In a fine mess, that's where."

Darcy blushed at the compliment. The men murmured their approval and William grinned widely at her from where he was crouched stroking the ewe.

"Aye, we would indeed," Quinn said, so softly she barely heard the words. "And me especially."

She looked at him sharply and found his eyes fixed on her. Her heart began racing. To cover her sudden discomfort she turned to the basin and washed her hands and forearms in the cold water.

Old Mac and William filed out, leaving Darcy alone in the kitchen with Quinn. She nearly jumped out of her skin when he stepped up beside her.

"You shouldn't sneak up on people like that," she said. "You could have given me a coronary."

"A what? Never mind. Sorry."

He was doing it again. Staring at her. Staring with that look in his eyes. The one that made her breath come in sharp little gasps.

"Ye have my thanks for what ye did today," he said. "And the thanks of the whole clan."

"Me?" she said. "I didn't do anything. You were the one who waded across a river to save the flock."

He shrugged as though this was unimportant. "We might have lost some of those sheep without ye. We certainly would have lost the injured ewe. I've never seen the like. Old Mac is right: ye are a marvel. I've always known it. Right from the moment I first found ye."

"Just doing my job," she mumbled, heat rushing into her cheeks.

"Well, thank ye all the same."

"Your help was invaluable," she said. "You'd make quite the veterinary nurse."

He snorted a laugh. "I take it from that grin on yer face that's an image that amuses ye?"

"Yeah, I can picture you in the uniform. You'd look quite fetching."

"Fetching is it? Ye flatter me, lass."

All of a sudden Darcy was painfully aware of how he stood less than an arm's span away from her. Before she knew what she was doing, she reached out and ran a finger down his bicep. He went very still, watching her with those piercing eyes.

"You'll catch a cold if you're not careful," she murmured.

"It'll be worth it," he breathed.

His eyes locked with hers. "We make quite the team, don't we?"

"Yes," she whispered. "Quite the team."

Something seemed to shift between them. Darcy couldn't quite put her finger on what it was. It was as though a balloon had burst and the tension that had built between them suddenly leaked away. She found herself grinning. Quinn grinned back.

Old Mac stuck his head around the door. "Sorry if I'm interrupting," he said, "But the rain's getting worse. The lads and me are gonna get the flock to higher ground."

"I'll help ye," Quinn said, turning, but Old Mac laid a hand on his shoulder.

"Nae, lad, ye've done enough for us already." He glanced at Darcy. "And I think Lady Darcy could do with being escorted back to Dunbreggan."

"Aye, I think ye might be right." He held his hand out to Darcy. "My lady?"

Darcy took his hand.

"Let's get ye back to the castle, shall we?" he said. "I'm guessing ye would nae say no to a dry set of clothes and a warm bath."

"That sounds wonderful," Darcy agreed. "Though probably not in that order."

"Aye, yer right," Quinn laughed. "If ye'll let me, I'll escort ye back to Dunbreggan."

They set out, Quinn walking so close by her side their elbows were almost touching, William running ahead, splashing in puddles. They walked in silence but it wasn't an awkward one, for once. It was companionable and Darcy felt herself feeling more relaxed than she had in days, weeks, even. She glanced over at Quinn and found him looking at her.

He smiled, a warm, friendly smile and she found herself grinning back. Then, for no reason she could name, she burst out laughing. After a moment, Quinn did the same. She loved hearing him laugh. It was a deep rumble that seemed to echo in his chest. It was like a rare jewel that lit up the day with its beauty.

Quinn laughed for the pure joy of it. For a job well done, for a worthwhile task completed. But most of all he laughed for the joy of having this wonderful woman at his side.

He'd been an idiot. A damned fool. He'd tried to deny his feelings, tried to put the clan first. It hadn't worked. Today had proven that. Darcy drove him crazy half the time but that only made him want her all the more. He'd never felt more alive, more complete as he had today as they'd worked together to save Old Mac's flock. A team.

The words of Irene MacAskill suddenly came back to him. *Ye'll have a choice to make. Make sure you make the right one.*

Was this the choice she'd been talking about? Should he choose to risk his heart on this woman? This woman who might leave him and go home?

Yes, he'd take that risk. She might reject him. She might leave him. But he had to try. He had no choice. Perhaps he never had.

He turned to look at her. Even with her hair and clothes plastered to her, even with rain running in rivulets down her face, she still stunned Quinn with her exotic beauty. But it wasn't her looks that made her wonderful. It was her fire, her spirit, her wit and skill. What she'd done today was nothing short of miraculous. He'd never met a woman like her before. Everything she did confounded him. Everything she did left him scratching his head.

But everything she did also filled him with fire and made him feel alive.

The village loomed ahead. William gave them both a hug and then pelted off towards his father's house, already shouting out his news. No doubt Darcy would be a hero out of legend by tonight.

He smiled. So be it. His she-wolf deserved such accolades.

They crossed the causeway together and approached the open gates of the castle. Quinn found himself wishing the end of the causeway would never come. When it did Darcy would disappear up to her room and he'd be without her. Then the strictures of his position would keep him from her side. He had so many duties pulling at him.

No, he told himself. *I've made up my mind. Darcy will be mine. If she'll have me. No more of this nonsense about duty.*

They paused on the steps. The rain was still pelting down and the only people visible were the guards on the battlements. Quinn took Darcy by the shoulders and turned her to face him. She didn't resist. She stared up at him, her eyes wide, her lips parted.

"Darcy, I-" he began. Why was this so hard? Why did words never come easily to him? He tried again. "I want to apologize. Ye know, if I've been a little...difficult..." he trailed off.

Darcy raised an eyebrow. She wasn't going to make this easy for him.

"What I mean to say is...after that kiss at the forge...well, I kept away from ye. Not because I didnae want to see ye. Lord help me, I wanted that more than anything, but because I didnae want to ruin things. I didnae want ye thinking badly of me. I didnae..." he threw up his hands. "Oh, I didnae know why I did it!"

Her big brown eyes seemed to draw him in. "Quinn, what are you trying to say?"

He didn't have the words. If he tried to explain he'd only make a mess of it so he did the only thing he could think of.

He kissed her.

As his lips touched hers fire exploded in every nerve of his body. The ache in his groin became almost painful. He pulled Darcy close to him, encircling her in his arms, pressing her against his chest. She melted into his arms and their kiss deepened. Darcy's lips were soft and warm. And hungry.

Arousal flared through Quinn as Darcy curled her fingers into his hair, moaning softly against his mouth. Lord help him, but he wanted her. He wanted to lay her down right here and take her. Make her his. He wanted to-

"Well that's not something ye see every day."

Quinn and Darcy jumped apart.

Rebecca was standing on the top step, looking down at them with a wicked grin on her face. "Here's me getting worried about the both of ye when it looks as though ye've both been having the time of yer lives!"

"Rebecca I-" Darcy said, just as Quinn said, "Ye shouldnae have been watching!"

Rebecca waved away their hasty words with a laugh. "Look at the two of ye! Like naughty children been caught with their hands in the cake tin! Ye dinna need to worry, half the clan have been taking bets on when this would happen!"

Quinn found a stupid grin spreading across his face. He looked at Darcy and found she was grinning too.

"Well, are ye gonna come inside or not? Ye'll catch yer deaths standing out there!"

Quinn took Darcy's hand and led her into the hall. A servant was waiting with two thick blankets which she threw around their shoulders. Rebecca took charge. With a few swift words she sent servants running to prepare baths. She took Darcy's arm and steered her towards the stairs.

"Ye can see Darcy later. I'll not let it be said that any guest of mine died of a chill! Then, when ye've recovered a little, we are gonna celebrate! Come on!"

Darcy looked over her shoulder as she was herded across the hall. The look she gave him set Quinn's heart on fire.

Later, that look said. *Later.*

Chapter 13

Light streaming through her bedroom windows woke Darcy the next morning. She opened her eyes, squinting, to see Alice pulling back the drapes.

She groaned and turned over, burying her head in the pillow. "What time is it?"

"Nearly the third hour after dawn, Lady Darcy," Alice replied "Lady Rebecca said I should let you sleep in after yer day yesterday."

Sleep in? Darcy said to herself. *It's barely seven o'clock!*

"Thank you, Alice," she mumbled. "I'll get myself ready. Tell Rebecca I'll be down shortly."

Alice nodded and crossed to the door. She paused before leaving and looked back at Darcy. "Is it true?" she asked.

Darcy sat up, wrapping her hands around her knees. "Is what true?"

"That in America there are women warriors and chieftains and that a woman can do whatever she pleases, even if her menfolk don't approve?"

The look of wonder on Alice's face made her smile. "Yes, Alice, it's true."

Alice's smile grew. "I'll tell Lady Rebecca ye'll be down anon," she said before slipping out and closing the door softly behind her.

Darcy threw back the covers and padded over to the window. The sky was blue and clear, the sun shining down. The large puddles that dotted the courtyard were the only indicator of the downpour yesterday. A twinge of guilt stabbed at Darcy. The clan was up and about, everyone already going about their day, and here she was sleeping late! She washed and dressed then pulled open her bedroom door and halted in surprise.

A bunch of meadow flowers lay on her doorstep.

They were tied with a red ribbon – tied with clumsy fingers that made the bow a big messy knot. She had no doubt who they were from. With a little cry of pleasure she scooped them up and held them to her nose. The scent reminded her of summer – and of Quinn. His scent seemed to be the smell of the Highlands themselves – clean air, sharp wind and the grasses that blew in that wind.

Ah, Quinn.

What was she to do about him? He'd filled her dreams all night. Those piercing eyes, that chiseled face, those strong arms. Yesterday had changed something between them. Darcy wasn't entirely sure what. She only knew that something was growing inside her. Something dangerous. If she gave into it, she would lose herself. Lose herself in him. But wasn't she going home soon?

She placed the flowers on her dressing table – reminding herself to ask Alice for a vase – and hurried downstairs to the great hall. She was disappointed to find it almost empty. There was no sign of Quinn, Laird Robert or any of the warriors. A few servants were sweeping the floor and Rebecca was seated at the head table with the steward, looking over parchments laid out on the table before them.

"Morning, sleepy!" Rebecca called. "Come on over and join us."

Darcy held up a hand. "I don't want to interrupt, you look busy."

Rebecca pulled a face. "Ye can interrupt all ye want. If I read one more account of drainage problems in the southern meadows, I swear I'll fall asleep!"

The old steward, a man named Jamie, rolled his eyes at Rebecca. "And here's me thinking I'd finally impressed on ye the joys of estate management."

"Oh, I'm sorry," Rebecca said, eyes going wide and putting her hand to her mouth. "I didnae mean *ye* are dull of course, Jamie, just that we've not talked of the most interesting of subjects have we?"

Jamie's eyes twinkled with merriment. "Aye, that we haven't. Well, mayhap it's time we took a break. My old bones could do with a rest by cook's fire and a mug of her finest brew. These damp days make my bones ache." He climbed slowly to his feet. "If ye ladies will excuse me?"

He gave a little bow and then disappeared through the doorway that led to the kitchen. Rebecca swept aside some of the parchments and patted the seat next to her. Darcy slipped into it.

"Well, ye look like ye slept well."

"I did," Darcy agreed. "I hadn't realized I was so tired."

"And who can blame ye with all the fuss last night? I hope the clan didnae overdo it. They can be a little... excitable at times."

Darcy laughed, leaning against the wooden back of her chair. "I really enjoyed myself," Darcy said, remembering the singing and the dancing. "Everyone was so kind. I can't thank you enough for everything you've done for me."

Rebecca waved away her thanks. "I'd say ye have repaid our hospitality many times over." She clapped her hands and Alice stuck her head into the hall. "Fetch Lady Darcy some breakfast will ye? I'll bet she's hungry enough to eat a horse."

As Darcy ate, they fell into easy companionship. Rebecca chatted – well gossiped really, albeit good-naturedly – about the goings on in the clan. Lily's new cloth had gone down a storm. Half the clan warriors had ordered new plaid from her and she was so busy she'd had to place a second order of cloth from her Flemish supplier. There were rumors Old Mac was planning on asking Annie Dunbar, a widow who lived with her daughter, for her hand in marriage.

Rebecca seemed to know everything about everyone and it wasn't long before she got around to the subject Darcy had been dreading.

"He's not here," she said, raising an eyebrow at Darcy.

"Who?" Darcy said, trying to sound nonchalant.

Rebecca rolled her eyes. "Quinn, of course. Did ye think I hadnae noticed how ye keep looking up every time the door opens?"

Darcy blushed. "Do I?"

Rebecca patted her companionably on the arm. "He'll be back soon, nae doubt. He dragged Robert and the men out of bed at the crack of dawn this morning so they could start their training. No doubt so the rest of his day will be free for other things. Did ye like the flowers?"

"You know about the flowers?"

"Aye. He asked my advice before he went down to the meadow to pick them. He might be a brave warrior and a fine leader of men but when it comes to the gentler arts, our Quinn can be a little clueless."

"I loved them," Darcy said. "They're beautiful." She found herself suddenly spilling out words. "I hadn't expected it. I didn't think Quinn liked me like that. He always seemed to find me...exasperating."

"And no doubt he still will," Rebecca laughed. "But that doesnae mean he canna find ye attractive as well. And judging by what I saw on the step last night, he certainly does that."

Darcy shook her head. "This has all happened so quickly," she confided in Rebecca. "I...I'm a little overwhelmed."

"Do ye feel aught for him?"

"Yes!" Darcy said vehemently. "But it's not that simple."

Rebecca nodded. "Aye. The best things rarely are."

At that moment the door to the great hall opened, letting in a gust of air that sent the candles fluttering. Quinn and Robert walked in, Robert talking animatedly whilst Quinn listened. Both men wore swords strapped across their backs, fresh from the training yard.

They approached the two women and Robert leaned down to give his wife a noisy kiss on the cheek. "I see ye've chased Jamie off already then? I told ye you'd soon get bored."

Rebecca frowned at her husband. "Nonsense. Jamie and I have been working all morning whilst ye boys have been playing at swords. Isn't that right, Darcy?"

"That's right," Darcy muttered, barely hearing Rebecca's words. She had eyes for nobody but Quinn.

He took a seat next to her. "Are ye well?" he murmured. "How was yer night's sleep?"

"Fine. Good. Thanks for the flowers."

He fixed her with a look that made her heart flutter. Slightly out of breath, slightly sweaty from training, his hair falling in tousled locks onto his shoulders, he was so handsome it stole her breath.

"Yer most welcome. I'm glad ye slept well," he said. "I need ye fresh and rested today."

Darcy raised an eyebrow at him. "Whatever for?"

Quinn glanced at Rebecca and Robert who appeared to be chatting amongst themselves although Darcy had no doubt they were listening to every word. "I was hoping if ye've nothing better to do if ye'd like to come riding with me."

"Riding?" Darcy said.

"Aye," Quinn frowned. "But if ye dinna fancy it, if yer tired or whatever-"

"I'd love to!" Darcy said, cutting Quinn off.

The smile that lit Quinn's face made her heart soar. He took her hand and pulled her to her feet, curling his fingers gently round hers.

"Ye take care of our Darcy, ye hear?" Rebecca called after them as Quinn led Darcy towards the door.

Quinn glanced back over his shoulder. "Dinna worry, lass. I intend to."

Two horses were saddled and ready in the stables. One of them was Silver, Quinn's enormous warhorse, but the other was a beautiful chestnut mare with a flowing mane. Darcy looked her over with appreciative eyes, unable to stop being the vet.

"She's stunning," she breathed.

"Aye. Barley's her name. I hope the two of ye will get on."

One of the stable boys held Barley steady whilst Darcy swung herself into the saddle. Quinn climbed into Silver's saddle with the practiced ease of someone who's spent his life in the saddle. With a tug of the reins, they set off, heading out of the castle gates and walking the horses side by side along the causeway.

It promised to be a glorious day. The sun was already hot and shimmered off the loch like a million little fireflies. Yesterday's rain was starting to evaporate and pockets of steam rose from the hills. It wouldn't be long though before it burned off completely, leaving a beautiful sunny day. At the end of the causeway they turned north, away from the village, hugging the banks of the loch. In this direction the land turned more rugged and there were very few crofts visible. Dunbreggan was soon out of sight behind them. They could have been the only people in the whole world.

They rode in silence to the accompaniment of the singing of birds in the heather. Relaxation began to flood through Darcy's limbs. She let out a contented sigh.

"Ye all right, lass?" Quinn asked.

"Mmm," she said, a little dreamily. "I was just thinking how beautiful this place is. You have a wonderful home."

"Aye, I do." He fiddled with his reins for a moment. "And yer home? What's it like?"

Darcy thought for a moment. The traffic, the high-rises, the bars and cafes and restaurants. It felt a million miles and a million years away from here.

"My home is an amazing place. It's full of life and busyness and opportunity. But it's also a bit crazy as well."

"Do ye miss it?"

She met his gaze. "Yes. Sometimes. But not as much as I expected."

"And yer kin folk? Will they nae be worrying themselves sick over ye?"

"My friend Gretchen will, no doubt. She'll have the police out by now I'd wager. I wouldn't put it past her to come to Scotland herself looking for me!"

Quinn snorted. "That's all we need, another fierce American to deal with. One is quite enough for me."

Darcy raised an eyebrow. "Oh, I'm not that bad when you get to know me!"

She'd meant it as a joke but Quinn seemed to take it seriously. "Aye, I know that," he said. "Not too bad at all."

He was looking at her that way again. The way that made her heart lurch and sent shivers down her spine.

"We'll turn inland," he said. "It's easier riding that direction although we'll lose sight of the loch."

"Don't go easy on my account," Darcy said. "But if you'd like an easier route yourself, you only have to say so."

"Me?" Quinn said indignantly. "I was thinking of ye. I'm wasnae sure how good yer horsemanship is."

"Don't you mean, 'horsewomanship?' And my riding is just fine, thanks."

Quinn snorted but said nothing.

Darcy frowned. "What?"

"Nothing."

"Quinn MacFarlane if you've got something to say then say it."

It was his turn to raise an eyebrow at her. "Yer riding style – it's unconventional."

She looked down and realized that her gown had ridden up past her knees and showed an indecent amount of bare thigh. These dresses were not designed for riding. No doubt the women of this time rode side-saddle or something equally ridiculous. Well, she'd be damned if she was going to do that.

"Unconventional equals fantastic where I'm from. Care to put it to the test?"

Quinn seemed to be hiding a smile. "What do ye propose?"

"A race. First to that rock over there wins. What do you say?"

"I dinna think-"

"Yah!" Before Quinn could finish the sentence Darcy set her heels to Barley's flanks and sent her racing off down the beach. She crouched low in the saddle, standing in the stirrups, feeling the rush of wind on her hair.

After a moment she heard Quinn curse and risked a glance behind. He was thundering after her, a fierce look on his face.

"Yer mad, lass! Do ye know that?"

"I thought we'd agreed I was unconventional?" she yelled back.

"Aye! That too!"

Darcy laughed and turned her attention back to her mount. With a cry of exhilaration she nudged her to greater speed. The beach flew by underneath the mare's hooves and Darcy's hair went streaming out behind her. A flock of seabirds scattered into the air and Darcy whooped aloud at the sheer exhilarating joy of it.

Quinn pulled abreast of her and she could see that he was grinning too, his eyes alight with excitement. "I thought ye said you were a good horsewoman!" he shouted. "My old grandmother could do better than this!"

"Oh do you think?" she yelled back. "Eat my dust, Quinn MacFarlane!"

She urged Barley to greater speed. Neck and neck, the horses' shoulders almost touching, Darcy and Quinn raced across the sand. The horses whinnied, enjoying the ride as much as their riders. Sand flew from beneath the horses' hooves. The wind tore at Darcy's clothing and squeezed tears from the corners of her eyes.

The rock was getting closer. If she could just reach it ahead...

She pressed herself flat against Barley's neck and released the reins, giving the horse her head. With a shrill whinny Barley bunched her muscles and put on a burst of speed that had Darcy clinging desperately to the saddle. She burst past the rock a good five paces ahead of Quinn.

Darcy punched her fist into the air, letting out a whoop of triumph. She grabbed the reins and pulled the horse into a canter, a trot and finally to a halt. Quinn reined in beside her. For a moment they just sat there, grinning like children, chests heaving.

"So?" Darcy asked. "Do you acknowledge I'm the better rider? I won the race after all."

"Ye cheated!" Quinn spluttered. "Ye were off and running before I could even take breath!"

Darcy shrugged. "I never said I was fair, did I?"

"Nae, lass, ye didnae," Quinn said, holding up his hands in surrender. "I acknowledge yer win though it does hurt my manly pride to say so."

He swung a leg over the saddle and dropped onto the sand, pulling the reins over the horse's head and patting the beast's lathered side. "Did ye enjoy that, boy? Would ye like to go riding with Lady Darcy more often?" He looked at Darcy. "He says, aye, he would."

Darcy swung out of the saddle. "What's that, Barley?" she said, leaning close to the chestnut mare. "You'd like to go riding with Quinn more often? Well, that's settled then isn't it?"

Quinn grinned. "Certainly is. We canna argue with the beasts now can we? Though we'd best let them get some rest after such exertion."

They led the horses to the edge of the beach where it gave way onto the heather-cloaked hills on the other side. They rubbed down the horses, and tethered them on long lines. Quinn opened his bulging saddlebags and took out two nose-bags which he filled with oats. The two horses were soon happily munching away.

Darcy found herself looking out over the water. True to her prediction, the rains from yesterday had evaporated and now the sky was an uninterrupted blanket of blue. The light was so bright Darcy had to squint to look at it. She turned to face south. Somewhere down there was the stone arch and her way home.

"What are ye thinking, lass?"

Quinn moved so quietly she hadn't heard him come up beside her. He was standing close, his arm almost brushing hers.

"Nothing, really. Just about how strange fate can be sometimes."

He grunted. "Ye'll get no argument from me on that score." He looked out over the loch and Darcy surreptitiously watched him from under her eyelids. He had a faraway look on his face, as though his thoughts had suddenly flown far away.

"My turn," Darcy said. "Tell me what you're thinking."

"Oh, just wondering how I'm gonna stop ye telling the clan about how I lost to ye in that horse race. I have a reputation to protect after all."

"No chance!" Darcy said. "By the time I'm finished with you, your reputation will be in tatters!"

"Is that so?" he said, narrowing his eyes at her. "Then maybe it's time I showed you who's boss?"

Quick as a flash he scooped Darcy up and threw her over his shoulder. Darcy shrieked.

"Put me down you great oaf!"

"Not until ye promise to keep quiet!"

"No deal."

"Fine."

He set off across the beach towards the loch. Darcy alternated between laughing and shrieking as she bumped along on his shoulder, slapping at the hard muscles of his back to little effect. They reached the water's edge and Quinn halted.

"Well?" he said. "Do ye acknowledge that ye cheated?"

"Never!" Darcy yelled.

"It pains me, lass, it really does but I'm afraid ye've left me no choice. A dunking it is for ye."

He grabbed her around the middle and hoisted her into the air.

"Wait!" she shrieked. "Okay! You win! I cheated! I won't tell anyone I won!"

"Do ye promise?"

"I promise! Now put me down!"

Quinn lowered Darcy onto the sand. "See that wasn't so hard was it? I knew I could tame ye, lass."

"Tame me?" she cried indignantly. "We'll see about that!"

She darted forward, hooked her leg around Quinn's and neatly tripped him the way she'd been taught in self-defense class. Quinn gave a strangled yelp and went tumbling into the water. But at the last minute his arm snapped out, grabbed Darcy's wrist, and pulled her in after him.

Darcy went under with a splash and came up coughing and gasping. The water was freezing! She felt Quinn's arm go round her waist and suddenly he was pressing her close against his body. The water only came up to their waists and Darcy found her feet, leaning against Quinn and shaking water from her hair.

"That was unfair!"

"Did I ever say I was fair?" Quinn replied, throwing her own words back at her.

She looked up to find his eyes fixed on hers. She went very still. Even though she was soaked and freezing, a sudden warmth seemed to steal through her. She was suddenly very aware of Quinn's chest pressed against hers, of his arms around her back.

"Quinn I -"

He didn't let her finish. He bent his head and kissed her. Darcy's eyes slid closed. Her arms went around his neck, pulling him closer. The world seemed to recede until there was only Quinn. Only him. His lips became harder, more insistent against hers. His kiss was hungry, raw, full of need. His tongue circled her lips and then pushed into her mouth. With a moan, Darcy sagged against him and parted her lips, inviting him in. The hardness pressing against her belly spoke of Quinn's arousal and it sent a matching heat flooding through her from the tips of her toes right up into the crown of her head.

Too soon Quinn broke off the kiss. He stood looking down at her, breathing quickly, a slight flush in his cheeks. His eyes had gone dark, full of lust.

"Come," he said, taking her hand. "We'd best get dry. We'll catch our death if we stay in here much longer."

Darcy nodded dumbly and allowed him to lead her from the water and onto the beach. They returned to the horses and took shelter in front of a tall hillock.

Whilst Darcy seated herself and did her best to calm her thumping heart, Quinn collected a pile of driftwood from the beach and quickly started a fire. Even though it was a warm day, Darcy was mighty glad for the extra heat. She moved as close to it as possible, letting it dry out her sodden clothes.

Quinn seated himself cross legged next to her. He picked up a twig and began shredding it, throwing the pieces into the fire. Darcy wished he'd kiss her again.

Quinn MacFarlane did something to her. His calm strength, his complete confidence in his own abilities, his amazingly gorgeous body. She'd never felt like this before. It was unsettling. But exhilarating too.

Wasn't it just her luck that she'd have to travel back to sixteenth century Scotland to find a man like him? At first she'd thought him a standoffish macho male but she'd gradually begun to glimpse the man underneath that mask.

And she liked what she saw. A lot.

She shivered and shifted closer to the fire.

Quinn held out his arm. "Come here, lass."

Darcy scooted into the circle of his embrace, leaning against him whilst he wrapped his arm around her.

"I'm sorry. I should nae have pulled ye into the loch. That was a mean thing to do."

She looked at him incredulously. "Where I come from it's called getting a taste of your own medicine. I started it, remember."

"Aye, but yer not from around here and aren't used to the coldness of the loch. I should have thought of that."

"Is this a MacFarlane trait?" Darcy asked. "Or is it particular to you, Quinn?"

He frowned. "What do ye mean?"

"This habit of putting everyone else before you. Of taking responsibility for everyone else."

His frown deepened. "It's my duty to take care of the clan."

"Yes, but that doesn't mean you're responsible for every little thing. In my experience humans are tricky things that will do exactly as they please, whether you like it or not."

"Aye, I'm starting to realize that," he replied, raising an eyebrow at her.

Their eyes met. Something fluttered deep inside Darcy. Before she knew what she was doing she was reaching up, running a finger down his cheek. A shiver went through him and he inhaled sharply. Feeling reckless Darcy went up on her knees, cupped his face in her hands and kissed him.

Quinn went rigid for a second and then he was suddenly kissing her back. Kissing her with a wild, desperate need. His arms closed around her and with an animal-like growl he flipped her onto her back in the sand, his weight pinning her down.

His lips traveled down her neck, sending prickles of pleasure through her body. She tangled her fingers in his hair, her eyes sliding closed. She felt her nipples stiffen, pressing almost painfully against the fabric of her dress.

One of Quinn's strong hands reached up and cupped Darcy's breast, kneading the soft flesh. Darcy arched her back, gasping, as Quinn's kisses moved down her neck to the soft curve where neck met shoulder, trailing pure fire along her skin.

Quinn fumbled with the laces on the front of her dress and all of a sudden they came free, exposing her breasts to the air. Quinn bent his head and took one rosy nipple in his mouth, sucking and caressing. Darcy moaned, arching her back even further, fingers tightening in Quinn's hair.

One of Quinn's hands reached down, hiked up her gown and trailed a finger up the inside of her thigh. He nudged her legs apart and nipped at her breast hard enough to make her gasp. She reached under his plaid, running her fingers over the hard, contoured muscles of his back. She was rewarded when he shivered with pleasure. Her hands swept lower, feeling the round hardness of his backside, then underneath to where his manhood stood hard and proud from his body.

There was a deafening snort right above them and they both jumped as if a gun had gone off. Quinn rolled off her, reaching for his sword and Darcy pulled her dress back up, looking around wildly.

Something large loomed above them, blotting out the sun. It took a moment for Darcy's addled to brain to make sense of it but when she did she let out a relieved giggle. It was Silver, staring down at them with his ears pressed forward, his nosebag hanging askew.

"Beast, yer timing is impeccable," Quinn growled. He climbed to his feet, took the reins and led the horse away. "Go and pester Barley will ye and keep yer nose out of my business."

Darcy gathered her dress around her and climbed into a sitting position. Her heart was still thumping. She and Quinn had come so close to...

Quinn flopped onto the ground beside her. His hair was tousled, his cheeks flushed. It took all of her willpower not to reach out and kiss him again. Instead, she kept her mouth firmly shut and her hands firmly by her sides.

"I'm sorry, lass," Quinn whispered. His eyes still burned with lust but his voice was carefully controlled. "That was not wise. Can ye forgive me?"

"Forgive you? You do have some strange notions, Quinn. I believe I was a willing partner in what we almost did."

"Doesnae matter. I should know better. I almost dishonored ye and I canna have that. Ye deserve better."

"Okay," she said, laying her hand on his forearm. "You have my forgiveness if that's what you need."

He covered her hand with his. For a moment their eyes met and Darcy felt the stirrings of passion sparking between them again. Quinn pulled his hand away and cleared his throat.

"Come on, let's get back to Dunbreggan before we both end up doing something stupid."

In short order they were mounted and riding south again. Darcy kept Barley slightly behind Silver so that she could watch Quinn as they rode. She loved the play of the light across the muscles in his arms, the way his body swayed with the movements of his horse, the way his long hair stirred in the breeze.

She knew they'd done the right thing by not taking things further. But that didn't stop Darcy wishing that they'd done the wrong thing instead.

Chapter 14

Dunbreggan was on tenterhooks. No matter where Darcy went she could sense the tension. The servants spoke in hushed whispers. The errand boys tiptoed around the place. The warriors paced with looks of concern on their faces.

The source of the tension was upstairs right now, sequestered with her midwives, laboring to give birth to the heir to the lairdship. Rebecca's labor had started in the early hours of the morning and now, well past dawn, she still struggled.

Darcy sat in the main hall next to Lily. Ostensibly they were working on one of Rebecca's gowns, taking it in around the waist so it would fit her better once the baby was born, but neither Darcy or Lily had their minds entirely on the task. If it was difficult for them Darcy could only imagine what the waiting must be like for Rebecca's husband.

Darcy glanced over to the fireplace. Sure enough, Laird Robert was still pacing. He'd been doing this all morning, prowling up and down in front of the fireplace like an old wolfhound. He seemed unable to sit, even for a moment. Everyone kept their distance from the laird, even Quinn. He sat alone at the head table, watching his brother.

Footsteps echoed on the stairs and all heads turned as one of the midwives entered the hall. The middle-aged woman wiped sweat from her brow and pulled down the sleeves of her dress which had been rolled to her elbows. She steadied herself on the wall and took a deep breath, obviously exhausted.

She smiled at Robert. "Yer wife has given birth to a healthy baby boy, my lord."

Laird Robert let out a whoop of joy. He bounded across the hall, gave the midwife a huge kiss on the cheek, and then pushed past her, leaping up the stairs two at a time.

"Ye should let her rest!" The midwife shouted after him. "Don't ye go tiring her out or ye'll be answering to me!"

"I'll be as gentle as a kitten!" Laird Robert's voice called back.

Lily pressed her hand against her chest. "That's a relief and no mistake," she said. "I'm so pleased for Robert and Rebecca. I know they both dearly wanted a boy."

"It's fabulous news," Darcy agreed, grinning.

With a laugh, she threw her arms around her friend and held her close. Already she could hear people shouting the news in the courtyard outside. It would be the talk of the clan in no time.

Darcy looked around for Quinn but he was no longer at his seat. She hadn't noticed him leave. She frowned. Where had he got to? She pushed back her chair and crossed the room to the warriors' table.

"Did any of you see where Quinn went?" she asked.

One of the men, a young lad barely out of his teens said, "I passed him crossing the bailey as I came in. He looked to be going round to the south tower, my lady."

"Thanks," Darcy replied. "And it's Darcy, not *my lady.*"

She crossed the hall and hurried down the steps into the bailey. She had a good idea where Quinn was heading.

Sure enough, as she rounded the south tower and came in sight of the tiny, fenced parcel of land that served as the MacFarlane cemetery, she saw Quinn's tall form outlined. He stood with hands clasped and head bowed.

Darcy slowed then halted a few paces away. She didn't want to intrude on this moment.

Quinn, though, seemed to sense she was there. He glanced over his shoulder. "Is everything all right, lass?"

"Yes," Darcy replied. "I came to find you. Are you okay?"

Quinn smiled wryly then held out a hand. Darcy hurried over and took it, leaning into him. Before them two wooden crosses marked the graves of Quinn's parents. Although he rarely spoke of it, Darcy knew he missed them. She knew how that felt.

"I come here when I need to think," he said. "It's peaceful. It helps to clear my mind. And I keep hoping my parents might offer some advice. They've not been too forthcoming so far."

"I do something similar," Darcy replied. "When I was a kid my dad would take me stargazing. We'd drive out into the hills and sit for hours, just staring up at the sky. Whenever I've got a problem, I do the same. Helps put things in perspective a little."

Quinn smiled. "My parents would have been very pleased to meet their first grandchild. Tis a great shame they're not here. Still, I'm sure they're watching from up above."

Darcy squeezed Quinn's arm. "I'm sure they are."

"I'm mighty glad the bairn's finally been born. I was beginning to fear he would never make an appearance. It's a weight off my shoulders and no mistake. I've been waiting for this moment ever since Duncan died."

Darcy wrinkled her brow, puzzled. "I'm not sure what you mean."

Quinn laid a hand on her shoulder. His eyes gleamed with joy. "Don't ye realize what this means? I'm not the heir to the lairdship anymore. It's been a millstone round my neck fearing I might one day have to take over from Robert. I was never meant to lead. I was meant for the blacksmith's forge and it's only a twist of fate that ensured the clan had to put up with me instead of Duncan."

"You're too hard on yourself," Darcy said. "You don't think you're a leader? Well I disagree. Your warriors worship you. They hang on your every word. And I don't know anyone who could have taken control of the situation over at Old Mac's farm the way you did. So you might not have been born to lead but you sure as hell learned to."

A faint, almost perplexed smile crossed his face. He reached out and gently ran the tips of his fingers down the side of Darcy's face. His hands were calloused, his skin hard from the days of hard work with a sword, but to Darcy it felt as soft as silk.

"Ye have a kind heart and the courage of a lion," he murmured. "Maybe that's why I love ye so much."

Darcy froze. Those words hung in the air between them. She must be dreaming. Had he really just said what she thought he did?

"Say that again," she croaked.

"Ye have the courage of a lion."

"No, the other bit."

"Ah, the other bit."

Quinn cupped her face in his hands and tilted her chin so she was forced to look deep into his eyes.

"I love ye, Darcy Greenway. I think I've loved ye since the moment I saw ye, even though I tried to fight it, fool that I am. Now it consumes me. I can hardly breathe, hardly think, and when I'm apart from ye it's like I've left a piece of me behind."

Darcy sucked in a breath to steady herself. She suddenly felt dizzy. She knew something had been growing between them. Something dangerous. Something wonderful. Now, at last, she recognized it.

"I love you too, Quinn," she breathed. "God help me but I do."

Quinn placed his forehead against hers and pulled her close. She could feel his heart thundering in his chest and realized he was as excited and nervous and terrified as she.

He gently pressed his lips to hers, kissing her as tenderly as if she were a piece of porcelain that might break.

"I'm so glad ye came into my life, Darcy Greenway," he whispered.

"Me too," she whispered back.

The breeze suddenly picked up, whirling around the castle with enough force to send Darcy's hair streaming out and her dress billowing around her knees. The wind sounded like a voice.

Choices, it seemed to whisper. *Choices.*

Darcy thought suddenly of the strange old woman who'd accosted her at the conference, Irene MacAskill. The old woman had told her she must make a choice and her heart's desire rested on making the right one.

Had she just made such a choice?

"Come on!" Quinn shouted against the wind. "Let's get back inside. Looks like the weather's turning. And I have a nephew to meet!"

Hand in hand, they returned to the castle.

The new bairn was named James Duncan after Quinn's father and elder brother. Quinn thought it a grand gesture to name him so. Right now, the two-week old James was staring up at Darcy as she gently rocked him. The lass was a natural with children, just like she was with beasts.

"He looks like you, Rebecca," she said.

"Do ye think so?" Rebecca asked from her seat by the window. "Most people reckon he has Robert's looks."

"I hope not!" Quinn laughed from where he sat by Darcy's side looking down at his nephew. "Robert has all the good looks of a fence post!"

Rebecca laughed. "I'll tell him ye said so! I'm sure he'll find a way to show his appreciation!"

"No need," Quinn said. "I tell him all the time."

A drum suddenly sounded outside. Rebecca leaned close to the window. "What's that? Somebody's riding up to the gates."

Quinn was on his feet in an instant. Sure enough, a horse was speeding along the causeway with reckless abandon. The warning drum atop the battlements sounded again.

"It's Fraser!" Quinn said, as he recognized the rider. "He's finally returned." He spun on his heel and strode to the door. "Ye two stay here. I'll send word as soon as we know what news Fraser brings."

He strode through the door, leaving the women staring after.

Dunbreggan was alive with rumor. News of Fraser's return had gone ahead of Quinn and the castle was abuzz with it. They all knew how important this could be. Quinn all but ran down the corridors and leapt up the stairs. Fraser had been gone for months and there had been no word. What news would he bring?

He reached the door to Robert's solar and pushed it open without knocking. Several men were gathered around the large table inside. Robert was seated but the rest stood, except for Fraser who sat opposite Robert, a blanket thrown across his shoulders, sipping a goblet of wine.

Their head's turned as Quinn entered.

"Brother," Robert said, waving him forward. "I'm glad yer here. I dinna reckon we could have waited much longer for Fraser's tale. Sit."

Quinn took a seat at Robert's side. Fraser looked up from his drink and Quinn's heart almost stopped. Fraser's right eye was black and swollen. Both nostrils were encrusted with blood. He held his left arm cradled against his chest as though it pained him. He'd obviously been in a fight and come out on the worst end of it by the looks of his injuries.

"Who did this to ye?" Quinn growled. "We'll see they pay dearly for it."

Fraser grimaced and gingerly put his cup on the table. "Ye should see the other man," Fraser said with a weak grin. "He'll nay be winning any beauty contests any time soon."

The men chuckled at Fraser's attempt at humor but Quinn and Robert didn't join in. Robert placed his palms flat against the table and leaned towards Fraser.

"It was a dangerous mission ye accepted, lad, and it looks as though that danger found ye. Tell us what happened."

Fraser swallowed thickly and began his tale. "It went well to start with. I took lodgings at an inn and pretended to be a merchant, selling Lily's cloth, just like we agreed. It took a while but eventually I got invited up to the castle to show my wares." His sharp blue eyes fixed on Robert. "It's as we feared. Laird Malcolm is dead and Merith, his only child, has married John de Clare. He's seized power and is laird in all but name."

Robert cursed softly under his breath. "This is nae the news we were hoping for. What of the clansmen? Have they accepted de Clare? Are they loyal to him? Is there any who challenge his rule?"

Fraser shook his head. "That's what I wondered at first. Surely there must be some of the Murray clan who wouldnae accept him, an outsider seizing control through marriage? Lesser things have caused rebellions. I asked around as secretly as I could, trying to gage opinion. I couldnae find any hint of dissatisfaction amongst the clan. It seems that de Clare has won them over by telling the Murrays exactly what they want to hear." Fraser's hand tightened around his goblet. "He's been stirring up the mob and no mistake. The castle and the villages were ripe with gossip about how de Clare had bested Duncan MacFarlane and how he would lead them to victory over their long-standing foes, the MacFarlanes, who've been raiding their lands and are busy raising an army to invade."

"That snake!" Quinn growled. "Duncan should have killed him when he had the chance!"

"Peace, brother," Robert said.

"Peace?" Quinn rounded on his brother. "Ye know what this man did!"

The death of his eldest brother at the hands of John de Clare was like an open wound in Quinn's soul. The fact that Duncan's murderer had gone free and now strutted around like a prize cockerel was a knife being twisted in that wound.

Robert laid a hand on Quinn's arm. Although his eyes were full of fire, his voice was calm. "We'll get revenge against de Clare, Quinn. Didnae we vow it on our brother's grave? But we'll nae gain anything if we allow our passions to rule us." He turned back to Fraser. "Carry on."

Quinn mastered himself with an effort. Robert always kept a calm head. That was why he made a better laird than Quinn himself ever could.

Fraser took a sip of his wine and then continued with his story. "I was in the main hall one night when a group of men came in. They weren't of the Murray clan although they were welcomed as such. I'm guessing they were de Clare's men. They brought a tale with them of a band of MacFarlane raiders harrying Murray lands to the north. They even sported cuts and bruises to show they'd been in a fight and had driven off the MacFarlane raiders."

"That's a lie," Robert said. "There havenae been any raids from our side of the border since before my brother Duncan's time."

"I know it," Fraser said. "But that's what the men claimed and the Murrays believed them. It was the final piece of evidence that de Clare needed to convince them. Now they're preparing to march against us."

A heavy silence fell in the room. So, it had come to this. Quinn had hoped that the long-standing animosity between the MacFarlanes and the Murrays would die with Laird Malcolm. It seemed that if John de Clare had his way that would be a vain hope.

"When?" Robert asked. "Where?"

Fraser shook his head. "I dinna ken. I'm sorry, Robert, but they caught me before I could discover their plans. One of the cooks reported me for asking too many questions and de Clare's men found me before I could make my escape. It was only with the aid of the innkeeper that I managed to get away at all."

Robert reached across the table and clapped him on the shoulder. "There's no need for apologies, lad. Ye've done well and because of ye we have some warning of what they're planning. Go and get some rest and I'll send up one of the healers and a servant with some food for ye."

"But I want to stay," Fraser protested. "If de Clare is marching on us I want to be a part of it when we ride out to meet him!"

"Ye will be, lad." Robert said, soothingly. "But right now yer nae use to anyone. Go and get some rest. That's an order from yer laird."

Fraser nodded reluctantly. He climbed to his feet and allowed one of the men to help him from the room.

"How long do ye reckon we have to prepare for any attack from the Murrays?" Robert asked after Fraser had left.

Quinn thought about this. He'd done many scouting missions along the Murray border and knew in detail the disposition of their settlements and forces.

"Tis a large area they control but much of it is upland and sparsely populated. With their people spread out the way they are it will take them a long time to gather their strength. I'd estimate a month at least before de Clare can gather enough men to march on us."

Robert nodded. "I agree."

He looked around at the men gathered in the room. Each one of them was strong and well trained and would die for clan MacFarlane if it came to that. "Lachlan, Dougal, you'll ride out tomorrow and deliver warning to our crofters and farms close to the Murray border. Ensure they make plans to evacuate as soon as they become threatened. Jamie, Connor, you'll ride out as well but I want you to begin gathering our outlying forces and bring them here to Dunbreggan."

The men who'd been addressed nodded, their faces grim and determined. "Yes, laird."

Robert turned to Quinn. "Brother, together we'll lead our forces. We've already set up messenger stations so we should get the word of the Murray's march long before they reach us. We must face them at a site of our choosing that gives us the best advantage."

Quinn stroked his chin. "Aye. I have a few ideas about that."

"Good. In the meantime, I'll dispatch messages to the other powerful members of the Murray clan and see if we can't talk some sense into them. If there's any possibility of ending this without bloodshed, I want to explore it." He looked around at his men once again and then nodded. "Very well. Ye all know yer tasks, let's get to it."

As Quinn left in a hurry, Darcy's immediate thought was Lily. Did her friend know that Fraser had returned?

Darcy handed James back to Rebecca, gave her a quick hug, and hurried from the room. She darted through the castle, across the outer bailey and then along the causeway. She reached Lily's shop and burst through the door to find Lily seated at her loom. Her friend looked up, startled, at Darcy's sudden entrance.

"Darcy?" Lily asked. "Is everything all right? You look as though you've just ran all the way from the castle!"

Darcy nodded, gulping in air. "I have. Or just about, anyway. I take it you've not heard?"

"Heard what?" Lily said, looking puzzled.

"Fraser's back."

The color drained from Lily's face. A heart-wrenching mixture of relief, hope, and anguish passed across her face. She took a deep breath and then turned back to her loom. "That's good. I'm glad he returned home safely."

Darcy stepped over to her. "Is that all you can say?"

"I have a plaid to finish for Rina Campbell. I promised I'd have it to her by tomorrow." Darcy noticed that Lily's hands on the loom were gripping so tight that her knuckles had turned white.

Darcy laid her hand on her friend's shoulders. "Don't you want to go and see if Fraser is okay?"

Lily shook her head. "It's not my place."

"Not your place?" Darcy cried indignantly. "He loves you! And you love him! It's about time you both stopped being so pig-headed!"

Lily frowned at her. "I've not come across that phrase before but I can guess from your tone what it means."

"Stubborn. Stupid. Ridiculous. Take your pick. Lily, come on." She grabbed her friend's arm and all but hauled her from the seat. "We're going to go and see Fraser, right now."

Lily didn't protest as Darcy locked up the shop and led her through the village to the castle. Already the place was abuzz with rumor. The servants gossiped in the hallways, the stable boys shouted to one another about war with the Murray clan and the warriors stalked through the castle with grim expressions on their faces.

They reached the door to Fraser's room and found it slightly ajar. The sound of voices came from the other side.

Lily halted. "He's not alone," she said. "What if Laird Robert's with him? I can't just go bursting in there!"

Darcy rolled her eyes. "Fine. I'll go and see who he's with. You wait here."

Lily nodded, waiting a few paces down the hallway. Darcy knew she shouldn't eavesdrop, but this was important. She wanted Lily to have the opportunity to be as happy as she herself was. And if that took a bit of meddling on Darcy's part, so be it.

She crept up to the open doorway and froze when she recognized Quinn's voice coming from inside.

"Nae, lad. Ye'll not be on the training yard for at least a day or two."

"But I feel much better. That potion the healer gave me has done the trick."

"Ye may feel better but that's deceptive. Yer injuries will take a while to heal. I'll nae risk ye hurting yerself further."

Fraser grumbled something under his breath. Then he changed the subject. "Seems things have been moving on a pace since I've been away."

"Aye. Robert and Rebecca's bairn has finally made an appearance and I'm glad of it. Twill be good to have a nephew to teach things."

"Aye, it will, but that's not what I meant."

There was a pause. Then Quinn said. "Nae? So what did ye mean?"

"Tales of ye and a certain bonny lass? The place is full of tales of ye and Lady Darcy."

Darcy's heartbeat quickened. She really ought to leave. Nothing good ever came of eavesdropping. Yet she found her feet rooted to the spot.

"So? Is it true?" Fraser prompted.

"Aye, lad," Quinn said softly. "Its' true."

"So, the famous bachelor Quinn MacFarlane has finally had his heart snared by a woman. It's like one of the romantic tales that the bards sing."

"Hardly," Quinn replied. "I canna say it happened like the tales. I had nae choice. I found her. I brought her here. She's my responsibility and I'll do my duty to her."

"So you're with her because ye reckon ye have to be?"

"Aye. She's a strange one with foreign ways. What was I to do? Nobody else would take her."

Darcy gasped, feeling like she'd just been slapped in the face. She caught herself on the door frame, legs suddenly weak.

Oh god.

He doesn't love me, she thought. *He's just trying to protect me out of some misplaced sense of responsibility.*

Her stomach churned so hard she thought she might throw up. Gritting her teeth, she forced herself to straighten, turn on her heel and return to Lily who was wringing her hands and all but hopping from foot to foot.

"Well?" Lily asked. "Can I go in?"

Darcy forced a smile onto her face. "Sure. He's with Quinn. They're chatting about unimportant things. Just go in. He'll be glad to see you."

Lily beamed. She gave Darcy a quick hug and then darted to the door. She knocked lightly and then pushed through it. Darcy paused only long enough to hear Fraser's exclamation of delight before spinning on her heel and hurrying away. She didn't want Quinn to catch her loitering out here. She had no idea how she'd react if she saw him. Fall to pieces or slap him hard enough to loosen his teeth?

She all but ran through the castle. Quinn's words kept replaying in her mind.

I had no choice. Nobody else would take her.

Each word was like a knife in her heart. She burst into her room and crossed to the wardrobe. She took out her medical bag and began stuffing all her belongings into it - the hairbrush Rebecca had given her, the few things she'd collected in her time here. When she had everything packed she changed into the jeans and boots she'd arrived in then quickly made her way upstairs to the library and took one of the maps she'd been studying. On it she'd marked where she thought the stone arch might be and she'd also marked a possible route that led to it.

She'd not been idle during the long weeks of poor weather and conflict with Quinn. However, her plan to get home had completely gone out of her mind since the rescue of Old Mac's flock and what had been growing between her and Quinn.

Stupid, she told herself bitterly. *Stupid, stupid, stupid. You don't belong here. You never did. What were you thinking?*

Rolling the map, she stuffed it into the medical bag and then quietly closed the door behind her. She crept through the castle, careful to avoid the busier corridors where she might bump into Quinn or Rebecca, and made it to the stables. Once there she asked one of the stable boys to saddle her horse which he did without question - they were used to her going out to see her patients in the nearby farms by now. She mounted quickly, tying her bag to the saddle behind her and kicking her horse into a trot.

Running away again, Darcy? she asked herself. *Yes!* she answered. *What choice do I have? I can't stay here. I can't stay with a man who doesn't love me.*

Without a backward glance she rode through the gates and out of Dunbreggan.

Chapter 15

Fraser grinned at Quinn, a mischievous look in his eyes. "So, the famous bachelor Quinn MacFarlane has finally had his heart snared by a woman. It's like one of the romantic tales that the bards sing."

"Hardly," Quinn replied. "I canna say it happened like the tales. I had nae choice. I found her. I brought her here. She's my responsibility and I'll do my duty to her."

"So you're with her because ye reckon ye have to be?"

"Aye. She's a strange one with foreign ways. What was I to do? Nobody else would take her."

He tried to make his voice sound authoritative. Fraser was a warrior under Quinn's command. It was important he saw his commander as strong, not as someone who had his head turned by a lass, no matter how true that was.

Fraser raised an eyebrow. "Yer duty?"

Quinn heard a sound outside the door. It sounded like the squeak of a floorboard. He almost went to investigate but when it didn't come a second time, he dismissed it.

"Aye."

"Ye really expect me to believe that?" Fraser asked. "I've nae seen ye so happy. Yer like a boy on his birthday! There's more to this than ye just doing yer duty to the lass!"

"I didnae say I wasn't going to enjoy that duty did I?" It was no good. He couldn't keep up the act. Quinn felt his stern warrior's mask crumbling and an idiotic grin spreading over his face. "My, but she's a fine woman, Fraser. I've never met anyone like her. She's turned my world upside down and no mistake."

Fraser nodded. "Aye, she's a special one all right. The question is, do ye love her?"

"Aye, I love her." It was surprisingly easy to admit that. Easier than he'd expected. In fact, just saying the words made Quinn feel invigorated. "I love the lass more than anything. I've never felt this way about anyone. Does that make me sound foolish?"

"Foolish?" Fraser snorted. "Nae, it makes ye sound human. It's about time ye found yerself a lass to settle down with."

He straightened in the bed, pushing himself more upright and fixed Quinn with a hard stare. "If there's one thing I've learned during my time among the Murray clan, is that ye must grab happiness when it comes yer way. Don't wait, don't question, grab it while ye have the chance because ye never know when ye'll get another one." He reached out and grasped Quinn's wrist. "If ye love her ye must ask her to stay and be honest about how ye feel. Trust me, Quinn. It's the only way."

Quinn opened his mouth to reply but was stopped by a knock on the door. A second later the door was pushed open and Lily's face peered around it.

Quinn smiled at Fraser. "What were you just telling me about seizing happiness when ye have the chance? Well, I think ye'd better follow some of yer advice." He stood, bowed to Lily, and made his way to the door. He paused at the threshold and turned back long enough to see Lily throw herself across the room and for Fraser to open his arms and welcome her into his embrace. With a smile, he left them in peace, quietly shutting the door behind him.

Fraser was right. He should tell her that he wanted her to stay, tell Darcy that he never wanted her to leave his side. He'd seize his chance at happiness, just like Fraser said.

But Darcy wasn't in her chamber. Nor was she in the great hall or the outer bailey, or anywhere else in Dunbreggan. He didn't find her in the village either and by the time he reached her empty clinic, he was beginning to get worried. Nobody had seen her. He returned to the castle and went back into her room. Closer inspection showed that her belongings were gone. The bag she always carried, the one she had with her when he first found her, was gone. The wardrobe had been stripped bare.

Fear ripped through Quinn. It was so hard and sharp it made him stagger and he caught himself on the windowsill. What had the fool woman done this time? Where had she gone?

"Oh," said a voice behind him. "What's going on?"

Quinn turned to find Rebecca standing in the doorway. She looked a little tired but otherwise healthy as her eyes scanned the room.

"Shouldn't ye be resting, lass?" Quinn asked.

Rebecca fixed him with a withering stare. "Don't ye start as well, Quinn MacFarlane," she growled. "I've taken enough of that from the midwives and Robert. I've had a baby, not a mortal injury. The next person to tell me to rest will regret it."

Quinn held his hands up. "My apologies. Where is my nephew?"

"He's asleep, thank the Lord. Robert is with him." She stepped into the room and looked it over, inspecting the empty wardrobe. "I heard ye were looking for Darcy."

"I canna find her anywhere. I must admit, I'm getting a bit worried."

"Have ye checked Lily's shop? The outer bailey? The great hall."

"Aye. There's no sign of her."

Rebecca frowned. "When did ye last see her?"

"A couple of hours ago. Shortly before Fraser returned."

"And ye havenae seen or spoken to her since then?"

"No, just Fraser and Lily when-" He trailed off as a thought came to him. "Come on," he said to Rebecca.

With a puzzled glance she followed him as he led the way back to Fraser's chamber. He knocked only once before pushing it open. Lily leapt up off the bed, her cheeks turning red and hastily brushing down her gown. Fraser looked annoyed at the interruption.

"Dinna worry, lass," Quinn said. "I'm not here to toss ye out. I just need to know if ye've seen Darcy."

"Yes," Lily replied. "She brought me here to see Fraser."

"So she was outside the room with ye?"

"She came to see who Fraser was talking to before I came in," Lily said, looking a little puzzled. "But she didn't stay for long."

A horrible suspicion was creeping up on Quinn. That sound he'd heard by the door. Could that have been Darcy? Had she been listening to his conversation with Fraser? How much of it did she overhear?

"What's wrong?" Rebecca asked, laying a hand on Quinn's arm.

"She's gone," Quinn croaked, suddenly certain of it. "She's left."

Lily's hands flew to her mouth. "Surely not!" she cried. "She wouldn't do that. Not after last time. She's happy here. What could possibly cause her want to leave?"

"I think she may have overheard something she shouldnae."

"But...but...she wouldn't leave. She doesn't know the land around here. Where would she go?"

The color drained from Rebecca's face. "She does know the land," she said.

"What do ye mean?" Quinn asked.

"Maps," Rebecca replied. "She's been studying our maps."

"Show me," Quinn commanded.

They left Lily and Fraser staring after and hurried upstairs to the map room. Once there Rebecca pulled out some of the ones Darcy had been working on. Two of them bore inscriptions in Darcy's neat hand and a route had been plotted from

Dunbreggan to a point on the shore of the loch - a point near where Quinn had first found her.

"She's trying to get home," he breathed. He snatched the map and then whirled on his heel.

"Where are ye going?" Rebecca called after him.

"Where do ye think? To find her. Tell Robert I'll be back as soon as I can!"

"Be careful!" Rebecca cried as he stalked through the door. "Ye know there are Murray brigands about."

"Aye, that's what worries me," he muttered.

He tore through the castle and out to the stables. The startled stable boys saddled his horse in quick time and then Quinn was up and mounted, galloping along the causeway and out into the countryside, following the route Darcy had marked on the map. His heart thundered in his chest. His hands were slick where they held the reins. He was terrified. More terrified than he'd ever been. If anything happened to Darcy...

He didn't finish that thought. He'd find her. He'd find her and bring her safe home.

Darcy found the route much easier going than last time. For one, the time she'd spent administering to the MacFarlane animals meant she knew the landscape much better than she did before. Secondly the weather was being kind and it was a clear day with a light breeze that made traveling easy.

And thirdly she had a map. That always helped too, of course.

Darcy made good time as she traveled south. She'd found the trail easily and now followed it along the contours of the loch shore, pausing every time she came across a fork in the path so that she could check her route. Early on in her journey she'd encountered other travelers and farmers working in their fields.

They all waved at Darcy and gave her a friendly greeting, no doubt assuming she was out on her rounds.

Each time she'd waved back, plastering a smile on her face, even though a lump formed in her throat. She'd never see these people again, these people who'd been so welcoming and accepted her into their hearts as though she was family. Each time she'd raised a hand and waved and whispered, "goodbye," under her breath.

After two hours of steady traveling she pulled the horse to a halt and dismounted, allowing her mount to graze whilst she stretched her arms over her head and worked the kinks out of her back. She took a sip of water from the leather bottle tied to the saddle. She'd not eaten anything since breakfast and in her haste to leave she hadn't bothered to pack any provisions. Still, it didn't matter. If all went to plan, she'd be stuffing her face in a twenty-first century restaurant in a few hours.

For some reason that thought filled her with sadness rather than excitement.

The horse suddenly raised her head and gave a whinny of recognition, her ears pricked forward. Darcy froze. A spike of alarm went through her. She scrambled back up the hillock to where she'd left the horse, heart thumping wildly.

Idiot! she chided herself. *What if it's those brigands again?*

But it wasn't. It was Quinn.

He'd pulled up his horse by her own and sat with his hands resting lightly on the pommel, watching her.

Darcy's heart thumped at the sight of him. She longed to run to him. She opened her mouth to call his name and then snapped it shut again. She brought to mind the words she'd overheard in Dunbreggan.

She's my responsibility. I'll do my duty to her.

The memory was enough to harden her resolve. She stood her ground, crossed her arms and stared at him, waiting. Silence stretched between them and neither moved. The breeze picked up, sending Quinn's black braids streaming out behind him. Slowly, he shifted his weight and, with the creaking of leather, swung one leg over the saddle and dismounted. He pulled the reins over his horse's head and stood there, holding them lightly in one hand. Still he said nothing.

Annoyance bubbled in Darcy's stomach. What was he doing here? Had he come after her out of his twisted sense of duty again? Did he expect her to babble her gratitude as though she was some weak-willed girl who needed his protection?

Well, if he expected her to speak first he could go to hell. If he expected her to do as he wanted, he could go to hell. She wouldn't do what he wanted any more. She was going home and there was nothing Quinn MacFarlane could do to stop her.

Quinn gripped his horse's reins to give his hands something to do. Otherwise he might just reach out and grab Darcy. He might pull her hard to him and hold her so close that she could never leave him again. But he knew instinctively that would be the wrong thing to do.

She stood only a few paces away but it may as well be a hundred miles. She wore that look on her face again. That fierce, determined look, that told him if he didn't tread very carefully he would pay a heavy price. So he just stood there, waiting for her to speak, knowing she wouldn't, and not being able to think of a damned word to say.

He'd ridden hard all morning. Darcy was no woods-woman and her trail was easy for any moderately trained tracker to follow. He'd not stopped to rest and his horse was lathered by the time he'd spied Darcy's own horse cropping grass in the distance. For a moment, sheer panic spiked through him as he spotted the horse rider less and then as Darcy emerged up the hillock, a strange mix of relief, joy and anger had enveloped him.

He'd thought it best not to speak. If he had, he wasn't sure what would've come out of his mouth. A tirade of angry words at her desertion? A hundred questions as to her welfare? Or would he have simply begged her to return with him, baring his soul in the process?

"Darcy," he said finally. "It seems I spend half my life chasing after ye. What are ye doing out here?" He already knew the answer to that question of course, but he had to say something to break the silent tension between them.

Darcy snorted. "Well I thought I'd take in the morning air. It's said to be good for your health." Her voice was heavy with sarcasm and Quinn winced. She wasn't going to make this easy on him.

"If it were yer health ye are worried about, riding out on yer own when there's brigands about isn't the way to help it."

"Is that so? Well, I think I'll take my chances. Now, if you'll excuse me, I'd best be on my way."

She took a step towards her horse but Quinn moved to block her path. She glared at him.

"I'd thank you to get out of my way."

Quinn held a hand. "Now, listen, lass-"

"If you're going to tell me what to do again, you can keep your god-damned mouth shut!" Darcy snapped. "I'm leaving."

"No yer not, lass," Quinn growled.

"And how are you going to stop me? Tie me up and throw me over your saddle?"

"Aye, if that's what it takes to make ye listen!"

"Try it!" she hissed. "I don't think you'll find it that easy."

Quinn scrubbed a hand through his hair and took a deep breath. This wasn't going how he wanted. "Listen, lass, please. I've ridden a long way to find ye. The least you can do is hear me out."

She narrowed her eyes and then crossed her arms again. "You've got one minute."

"Very well. But first, answer me one question. Why did ye ride out here? Why did you leave like that? Without even saying goodbye?"

"Because I have to go," Darcy replied. The defiance had gone from her voice and now it was filled with hurt instead. "Because I heard what you said to Fraser. I have a little self-esteem left, Quinn. I won't stay with a man who doesn't really want me."

Her words were like a sword thrust to his guts. The raw pain in her voice twisted his insides.

"Oh, Darcy," he said. "Ye should have come to me. Why do ye never speak to me about these things? Ye should have given me a chance to explain. If ye'd stayed perhaps ye'd have heard the rest of that conversation."

He risked taking a step closer and was pleased when she didn't back away. "If ye'd stayed ye'd hear me tell Fraser how my duty to you is no real duty at all. It's the opposite in fact. It's a joy because I love ye. I love ye so much it takes my breath." He shook his head. "When I learned ye'd left... I've never been so terrified in all my life."

"I...I..." Darcy stammered. She straightened her shoulders and glared at him again. "So why did you say those things about duty to Fraser?"

"Because I'm a fool. I'm a fool who tries to appear strong, even when I'm not. Even when I want to sing it to the world how I really feel about ye."

"And how is that?" Darcy asked.

"Lord, above! How many times must I say it? Do ye want me to shout it to the skies? Very well." He threw his arms wide, leaned back and bellowed in his best battle-voice, "I love Darcy Greenway!"

His words echoed off the rocks around them and seemed to take an age to fade into silence. Darcy's eyes went wide and he saw tears glittering in them. She came to him slowly, like a nervous animal and then gently laid her hand in his.

"I'm sorry," she whispered. "When things get tough I have a habit of running away. My bad. It was just hard to hear you say that to Fraser because I've loved you for a long time, Quinn."

The breath left him in a whoosh. It was such a relief to hear her say those words. He felt as though a weight lifted from around his neck. He took both her hands in his and kissed them. Then he leant down and placed his forehead against hers. This close he could smell her. That warm, beautiful scent that was uniquely her.

"Stay with me, Darcy. Forever," he whispered. "Say ye'll be my wife."

Darcy stared at Quinn, struggling to process what she'd heard. Had Quinn just asked her to marry him? She wanted to believe it. Good god, she wanted to believe it more than anything.

She opened her mouth and closed it again. Then tried a second time. "I..." she stammered. "I beg your pardon?"

Quinn cupped her face in his large, strong hands and looked down into her eyes with a gaze so intense it took her breath away. God, she could drown in those eyes of his.

"I said, will ye agree to be my wife, Darcy Greenway?"

So. It hadn't been a dream. It was real. This beautiful, strong, amazing man was asking her to be his. Forever.

Darcy began to tremble. She looked up into Quinn's eyes, although now she could barely see him for the tears swimming in her own.

"Yes," she whispered. "Of course I'll marry you."

A grin spread over his face and it was like the sun coming out from behind a cloud. Then he gave a whoop of delight, picked Darcy up by the waist and spun her round until they were both laughing and breathless. Only then did he put her down and she stumbled against him, her palms going against his hard chest.

One of his hands went round her waist to steady her, the other lifted her chin gently.

"Ye have no idea how happy ye've made me," he said, his voice hoarse with emotion. "I'll be a good husband to ye, love. I swear I'll spend my life trying to make ye happy."

Darcy nodded then reached up, tangled her fingers in his hair and pulled him down to kiss him. His arms tightened around her, pulling her against him.

A deep ache lit in her body, tingling along her nerves. She wanted him. Needed him. God, she wanted him more than she'd wanted anything.

Before she knew it, she was pulling him down into the grass and he followed eagerly. His hands explored her body, gently brushing down her back then along her sides. She grabbed his plaid and tugged, managing to get it over his head so his chest and shoulders were exposed.

"Are ye sure ye want this, love?" he murmured.

"I'm sure," she answered breathlessly.

It was all the permission he needed. He flipped her onto her back in the soft grass. His lips found her earlobe, gently licking and nibbling whilst his hand slipped under her top and the tips of his fingers circled her nipple. She gasped, arching her back as his grip hardened, caressing and kneading her breast, his tongue darting in and out of her ear.

He was good at this. Holy crap, he was good at this.

He pulled at her shirt and she obliged by yanking it over her head and tossing it away. Her bra went next and she lay back, skin prickling in the cool air. Quinn paused, his eyes roving over her bare torso.

"Lord, but ye are beautiful," he whispered. "So beautiful."

He bent his head and took a dusky pink nipple in his mouth. Darcy groaned, her eyes sliding closed as delicious sensations rippled through her body. Dimly a part of her worried that they were out in the open where anyone could see. But another part of her didn't care. She'd seen nobody for hours and the horses had wandered away up the hill to graze. There was nobody here but her and Quinn.

This was their place, their moment.

Quinn's hand roved lower, undid the zip of her jeans with an expert hand and slid down into her panties. The hard pad of his thumb found her sweet spot and gently began to caress the nub. Darcy jerked under him, screwing her eyes tight shut as something akin to electricity shot through her. She moaned and writhed, every nerve seeming to come alive.

Quinn grabbed her jeans and yanked them down. Darcy kicked them away, her panties following. Quinn's plaid was only tied round the waist and the sight of his semi-naked body sent Darcy giddy with desire. The way the plaid tented round his groin told her just how much he wanted her. She grabbed the knot that held the plaid and tugged it roughly. It tore a little as it came free but neither of them cared.

The plaid fell away and Quinn lay in the grass beside her. Darcy's eyes roved hungrily over his body. His manhood stood proud and straight, a thin sheen of sweat highlighting the contours of his thighs and the muscles of his stomach.

Almost hesitantly Darcy reached out and ran her fingers along the length of his shaft. His eyes slid closed and he moaned. Loving the power she held over him, she moved her hand, stroking him slowly, sensually, until his muscles were almost quivering with need.

"Ye must stop that, love," he said. "If ye carry on I dinna think I can hold off taking ye."

"Who says I want you to hold off?" she asked in a breathless whisper.

With a growl, he rolled on top of her, his weight pinning her to the grass. The heat of his skin against hers sent her pulse wild. She felt reckless and full of need. She ran her hands down the bare skin of his back, feeling the dips and ripples of his muscles.

He stared down into her eyes as he nudged her knees apart. The tip of his manhood bumped the spot between her legs and she tilted her hips towards him.

Slowly, eyes locked on hers, Quinn eased himself inside her. She welcomed him, tilting herself up to meet him, taking all of him deep inside. A breath hissed through his teeth and she felt his muscles bunch as he slowly began to thrust. It felt amazing. It felt...right.

She was consumed, lost in this man. In his smell, his presence, the sensation of his body atop and inside hers. For that moment, as he slowly made love to her on the soft grass, there was only him, only him in the whole world.

She moved in time with him, her hips rising to meet his thrusts, her hands caressing his back, one leg wrapped around his waist. Their tempo increased, becoming more urgent, more frantic. Little gasps of pleasure escaped Darcy as the fire burning inside began to increase, to rage into an inferno. Quinn growled each time he thrust, their bodies coming together in a tangled heat of passion.

"I love ye," Quinn whispered as he thrust deep inside. "I love ye."

It was too much. The fire ignited like gasoline, burning along Darcy's nerves, incinerating all thought. She arched her back, threw her head back and screamed Quinn's name into the sky as her climax swept her away. A moment later Quinn shuddered as he reached his own peak.

For a long, unknowable moment they just lay there, tangled with each other, Quinn still buried inside her. Then he rolled onto his back and pulled her into the crook of his arm. Fuzzy with sated desire, Darcy nestled against him, resting her head against his shoulder and throwing an arm across his hard chest.

"Well," she murmured dreamily. "That was worth waiting for."

A laugh rumbled in Quinn's chest and he kissed the top of her head. "There's plenty more where that came from, love."

"Hmm. I like the sound of that."

Quinn grabbed his plaid and pulled it over the two of them. Darcy snuggled closer, loving the sensation of his hot skin against hers, of the smell of him all around her. She could lay her forever. She drifted into sleep.

Some time later Quinn woke her with a kiss. He was lying propped on one elbow, watching her with a slight smile on his face.

"How long have I been asleep?" she asked.

"An hour or so."

"Why didn't you wake me?"

He shrugged. "I like watching ye sleep. Ye look so peaceful. Apart from the snoring of course."

"I don't snore!" she threw a mock punch at his shoulder.

With a laugh he caught her hand and kissed the back of it. "Oh ye do, lass. Loud enough to wake the dead."

Before she could respond he leaned forward and kissed her. Her indignation melted away. He rolled atop her and took her again, sweeping her away on waves of pure bliss.

The afternoon wore away. Darcy lost all track of time. It passed in a haze of swirling emotion and burning passion. She had no idea how many times they made love. She explored every inch of Quinn's body and he every inch of hers. Sometimes he was slow and gentle. Sometimes he was rough, claiming her with a primal need. But each time he was wholly Quinn, that heady mix of gentleness and brute strength that so intoxicated her.

At last, as the sun was falling to the horizon, Quinn let out a long sigh. "We'd best be getting back. They'll be worried about us."

So? Darcy wanted to say. *Who cares? I want to stay here forever. With you.*

But she only nodded. She sat up and reached for her clothes. Quinn watched her as she dressed. His eyes were full of hunger and admiration as his gaze roved over her. A sense of euphoria stole through her. When Quinn looked at her like that she felt like the most beautiful woman in the world.

When she was dressed she pulled him to his feet. He held perfectly still as she dressed him, wrapping his plaid around his waist and then his chest, like a wife would do before her man went into battle.

Unfortunately, they'd been so wrapped up in each other they'd forgotten the horses and the beasts had wandered off into the hills above the loch, looking for forage. It took the better part of an hour for Quinn to catch them. She sat cross-legged in the grass, chin propped in one hand and watched Quinn's antics.

She couldn't seem to stop smiling. She laughed at the way Quinn cursed and swore at the horses. She chuckled at the way the horses, sensing they'd got one over on him, allowed him to come within arms' reach before dancing away again. She smiled at the warm breeze that lifted her hair and drank in the beautiful sights and smells of the Highlands at dusk.

Eventually Quinn caught the horses and led them back to where Darcy sat. He raised an eyebrow at her.

"Dinna go breaking a sweat helping me, love," he said.

"You seem to have everything under control," she replied. "I wouldn't want to get in the way."

He shook his head in mock annoyance and then gave her a flourishing bow. "If yer ready, my lady, we'll be on our way."

"Certainly, my good man," she said. She allowed Quinn to pull her to her feet and then boost her into the saddle.

Quinn swung up onto his own mount and in moments they were moving back north, along the trail Darcy had fled what felt like a lifetime ago. The journey passed in a blur for Darcy. She was so engrossed in Quinn, in his nearness, his movements that she barely noticed the landscape they moved through. He seemed to be similarly affected as he started in surprise when they topped a rise and found themselves looking down on Dunbreggan.

By this time darkness was falling and lights twinkled in the village and the castle, sparkling in the waters of the loch. Darcy pulled her horse to a halt and sucked a deep breath through her nostrils.

"Are ye all right, love?" Quinn asked.

Darcy nodded. "I'm fine. Better than fine. It's just... The last time I left I didn't think I'd be coming back here." She looked at Quinn. "Thank you for coming after me."

Quinn reached out and squeezed her hand. "This is yer home now, love. Our home. Ye need never leave it again if ye so choose."

"My home," Darcy repeated. She liked the sound of that. She'd never really felt at home anywhere. Since her parents died she'd been adrift, looking for somewhere to belong. She never dreamed she'd find that place in sixteenth century Scotland.

Then a pang of guilt twisted her belly. What about the people she was leaving behind? Could she just abandon them? How would Doctor Andrews cope at the practice without her? And Gretchen? She was her best friend, the only person in all the world she could rely on. How could she abandon her?

"Darcy?" Quinn asked.

She squeezed his hand tighter. "I'll never see my folks again, will I?" she whispered.

A look of sadness flitted across his face. "I know how hard it must be to leave yer kin behind, love. But ye'll have new kin, new friends. And yer folks are welcome to visit anytime."

She smiled at him. She loved the way he tried to make her feel better. "You're right. And I look forward to having a new brother and sister as well as a new husband."

"Talking of said sister," Quinn replied. "We'd better hurry. I hate to think of the fury Rebecca will be in when she finds out we've given her worry for no cause."

Nodding her agreement, the two of them rode down the hill and into Dunbreggan. Sentries were posted on the walls to watch for their arrival so by the time they pulled up the horses by the main doors, Robert and Rebecca were on the steps waiting for them. Rebecca was nursing her infant son, wearing an expression that hovered between relief and annoyance.

As the two of them swung down off their mounts, Robert ran down the steps to meet them. He clasped hands with Quinn, forearm to forearm in the warrior way.

"I'm glad to see ye back, brother," he said. His eyes shifted to Darcy and he gave a grin very reminiscent of his younger brother's. "And I'm glad ye found our errant sheep and brought her back into the flock." He placed his hands on Darcy's shoulders. "Are ye all right, lass?" he asked. "Yer not hurt?"

Darcy's cheeks burned at his concern. If only he knew what she'd been doing all afternoon. "I'm fine," she stammered. "I...I...went looking for a trail I'd seen on a map. I didn't realize I worried you all."

Robert patted her shoulder. "Well, yer back now. That's all that matters. I suggest yer come and sooth my wife. She's been a little... fraught should we say."

Darcy nodded then made her way up the steps to where Rebecca waited.

"Where've ye been?" Rebecca demanded, rocking her son who was sound asleep. "Are ye well? Ye didnae run into any trouble? Did ye get lost out there?"

Darcy held up her hands. "Which question would you like me to answer first? I'm sorry, Rebecca. I didn't mean to worry you."

Rebecca frowned. "Well, ye must have gotten very lost if it's taken Quinn this long to find ye. He's the best tracker in the clan."

"Oh no," Darcy blurted before she could think better of it. "Quinn found me hours ago."

Rebecca's frown deepened. "So what have ye been doing all this time? Ye've been gone all day! I've been worried out of my wits!"

Darcy's cheeks flamed red. She opened her mouth but hesitated. What was she supposed to say? *Sorry, I got a bit delayed because Quinn and I have been making love all day?*

But Quinn came to her aid.

"Peace, sister," he said. "Darcy and I had much to talk of." He slipped an arm around Darcy's shoulder. "She's agreed to be my wife."

Rebecca's eyes went wide. One hand flew to her mouth which made a surprised little O. "But...but...that's wonderful!" she cried.

"Congratulations, little brother," Robert said, clapping Quinn on the shoulder. "It's about time. We all suspected it was coming with the way ye two moon after each other. I'm happy for yer." He leaned down and gave Darcy a kiss on the cheek. "Welcome to the family, sister."

"Here, take yer son," Rebecca said. She handed the sleeping infant to Robert then threw her arms around Quinn and Darcy both. "I'm so happy!" she cried. "A wedding to plan! No, wait a minute, two weddings to plan! The clan hasn't seen an occasion like this in many a year! It will be grand!"

"Two weddings?" Darcy asked. "What do you mean?"

Rebecca gave an impish little grin and then pushed open the door to the great hall. "Come and find out!"

The great hall was busy. Groups sat around at the tables, eating, talking, playing games of dice and cards. The hum of conversation filled the air. Darcy spotted Lily and Fraser sitting at the main table, heads together, talking quietly. Lily looked up at the sound of the door opening and she broke into a smile when she saw Darcy and Quinn standing there. She took Fraser's hand and they hurried across the hall towards them.

Lily, Darcy saw, wore a piece of Fraser's plaid attached to her shoulder.

"Darcy," Lily said breathlessly. "I'm so glad you're back. Are you all right?"

"I'm fine," Darcy said, waving away her friend's concern. She reached out and gently brushed the plaid pinned to Lily's shoulder. Both Lily and Fraser had a flush to their cheeks and both seemed unable to keep their eyes off each other. "Lily, what's going on?" Darcy asked.

Lily laughed and Fraser threw an arm around her waist and pulled her close. "We're going to be married," he said.

Darcy's jaw dropped. "That's fabulous! I'm so pleased you finally plucked up the courage to ask her!"

"It wasnae I did the asking," Fraser said.

Lily blushed, looking a little embarrassed. "I took your advice, Darcy. You have to seize happiness when you have the chance don't you? So I did. I asked Fraser if he'd agree to be my husband."

"And I said yes," Fraser finished. "I'd wanted to ask Lily for months anyway. She saved me the trouble."

Lily stepped forward and took both of Darcy's hands in hers. "I want to thank you," she said. "For everything you've done. Without you showing me the way, without your support I'd never have worked up the courage to do this."

Darcy squeezed Lily's hands and smiled. "And without you I'd have not had the courage nor the means to set up my practice. There's nothing to thank me for. That's what friends do for each other."

Rebecca rolled her eyes. "Honestly, ye two! Darcy, aren't ye going to tell them yer news?"

"What news?" Lily asked, puzzled.

Quinn stepped up and placed a hand round Darcy's shoulders. "Mayhap yer not the only ones to get betrothed on this day."

Lily looked from Quinn to Darcy and back again. "You mean...you mean...?"

"Yes!" Darcy cried, clapping her hands together. "Quinn asked me to marry him and I said yes!"

Rebecca stepped between the two couples. She wore that mischievous grin on her face again. "And ye know what that means don't ye?" She looked over her shoulder at her husband. "Robert, summon all the servants, rouse the cooks. We're going to have the biggest betrothal party this castle has ever seen!"

Chapter 16

Quinn awoke early as he always did. Light was beginning to filter through the windows and out in the bailey a cock crowed. Quinn stretched, enjoying the heavy feeling of contentment in his limbs. Beside him, Darcy snored softly. Her raven hair spilled across the pillow, one long, lean leg poking out from beneath the coverings. Quinn propped himself on his elbow and spent a few minutes just watching her sleep. Following their betrothal Darcy had moved into his room. Their room.

He still couldn't believe she was his. Mind, body and soul. Now all they needed was their wedding and she'd be his in the eyes of the Lord too. It couldn't come soon enough for Quinn.

He leaned down and brushed a stray strand of hair from her face and kissed her lightly on the forehead. Darcy shifted in her sleep but didn't wake. Nestled in the crook of her neck and bound by a thick cord was the ring he'd given her as a sign of their betrothal. It had belonged to Quinn's elder brother, Duncan, and Quinn had carried it since his death. He was glad to see it hanging around Darcy's neck now as a symbol of their union.

A boom sounded from outside, making Quinn jump. It was followed by a second and then a third. He waited for a fourth beat. *Boom-doom*. There it was, the signal drum atop the watchtower indicating a messenger had returned with news of the Murray clan's army.

Careful not to wake Darcy, Quinn climbed out of bed and threw on his clothes. The morning air still held a chill and sent goose bumps riding up his skin as he padded across the cold stone floor.

"Where are you going?" Darcy mumbled, her voice heavy with sleep.

"I have to see Robert, love. The message drum sounded."

"I'll come with you."

"Nae, lass. Ye sleep. I think I tired ye out a little last night."

"You sure did," she replied with a smile. "But I'm up for a little more 'tiring'."

He grinned and kissed her forehead. "Later, love. Ye go back to sleep. I'll be back before ye know it."

He closed their chamber door quietly behind him and made his way through the waking castle to his brother's solar. Robert was there already with the messenger standing before him. Fraser was there as well and Dougal and Rabbie.

Robert nodded to Quinn as he took a seat by his brother's side. The messenger was Finn MacGarrety, a lad of no more than sixteen summers who'd fostered with the MacFarlane clan when his parents were killed in a raid by the Murrays. Sweat dripped from the lad's brow and his face was flushed. Quinn wouldn't be surprised if the lad had ridden all night.

Robert poured a cup of wine and handed it over. "Drink, lad, get yer breath back then tell us yer news."

"My thanks," Finn said. He took the wine, gulped it down in one, then handed the cup back to Robert.

"It's grim news I bring, my lord. The Murray army is on the march. They will reach our border in two days."

Robert's expression turned dark. "Where?"

"East. They're coming up the old drovers pass past Oldwyn's Barrow. They're flying the banner of the Murray clan and John de Clare."

"Curse them," Robert growled. "If they reach the high ground around Oldwyn's Barrow they'll hold the advantage."

"Not necessarily," Quinn replied. "The land around Oldwyn's Barrow is moorland with thick peat underneath a thin covering of heather. With all the rain we've been having lately, it will be like a bog. They'll find it difficult to move with any speed on that terrain and if we reach it before them we can claim the Point."

"Aye," Robert said. He rubbed his chin, eyes narrowed in thought. "De Clare will only see the advantages of the high ground. He doesnae know our lands and won't know how boggy that area turns after rain. But the Point is limestone through and through. If we can get our forces there we won't be hampered by the terrain the way he will be. We'll have the advantage."

Robert's eyes shone. Quinn knew that look. Robert saw a chance for victory. A chance to end the threat of John de Clare once and for all.

And a chance to avenge the murder of their elder brother.

A savage glee arose in Quinn. He'd spent long hours on the training field, preparing both himself and his warriors for this moment. Now it was finally here and he would do his duty to his people. He would fight to keep them safe.

"Fraser, send word to our people in the east. Tell them to begin evacuating any of the crofters who lie in the path of de Clare's army and bring them here to Dunbreggan."

Fraser nodded. "Aye, lord."

Robert turned to Dougal. "Begin readying supplies and have the horses provisioned and prepared."

Dougal nodded. "Aye, lord."

Last, he turned to Quinn. "Send out word to rally our warriors. Have them gather here at Dunbreggan. We ride tomorrow at first light."

Quinn closed his eyes, pulled in a deep breath, then opened them again. He nodded. "Aye, lord."

Darcy wasn't sure if she'd ever felt more afraid. She stood with Lily and Rebecca and a few retainers and guardsmen who remained at the castle and watched the MacFarlane army ride across the causeway and then snake their way up into the hills beyond. She gripped Lily's hand on one side and Rebecca's on the other, so tight she must be hurting them, but neither complained.

Robert, Quinn, and Fraser rode at the head of that column. Despite her entreaties for him to keep himself safe, Darcy knew Quinn would be in the thick of battle. It was his duty. He'd fight to protect his brother, his clan, his people.

Their goodbye had been long and lingering. Darcy had said not a word about her doubts to her husband-to-be, instead trying to be brave, helping him don his battle gear and talking in a calm, clear voice about the welcome that would await him when he came home victorious.

All just words. All just bluster and she knew Quinn saw straight through her. The way he tenderly took both her hands in his and kissed them, his blue eyes full of concern, told her he realized how scared she was.

"I'll return to ye. I promise," he'd whispered. Then he'd pressed his forehead against hers, taken a few deep breaths and strode away from her.

The rest of the gathering atop the steps began to disperse. Rebecca went back inside to see to her son who'd started crying. Darcy and Lily stood and watched until the very last remnants of the army had disappeared into the distance.

"How long do you think they'll be gone?" Lily asked.

"Several days at least," Darcy replied. "Quinn says it's a long ride to the border, although they'll be pushing the horses hard to get there before the Murrays. After that?" She shrugged, trying to appear nonchalant. "Who knows?" She placed a hand on her friend's shoulder and forced an encouraging smile onto her face. "They'll return soon. Try not to worry."

Lily raised an eyebrow at that. "Yes, I'll try. But I have the feeling that trying won't get me anywhere."

Darcy squeezed her shoulder. "Me neither. Come on, the best way to take our minds off it is to keep busy."

Together the two women made their way through the village to Lily's shop. Customers were already gathered outside when they arrived. A mother and her daughter were there to try and pick out some new gowns and a shepherd was waiting with a ewe who'd gone lame. Darcy smiled wryly. The men may have ridden off to battle but life in the village went on as normal. There were still clothes to be sewn, animals to be cared for. Darcy was glad of that.

The next day proved to be equally busy. In her clinic Darcy swabbed the wound with antiseptic she'd managed to make from local ingredients since her own supplies were dwindling, then leaned down with needle and thread ready. The hound, one of the clan's prime hunting dogs, and the pride of the kennel master's eyes, lay unconscious on the table. Darcy had given him enough anesthetic to keep him out for the count while she stitched up the ragged tear in his shoulder.

A wild boar had caught the hound unawares while out on a hunting trip but luckily the animal had managed to escape before the boar could do any real damage. There was a bit of torn muscle and the dog would walk with a limp for a while but he should make a full recovery.

The door opened and the kennel master stuck his head around it. The ruddy-faced man looked worried. "How goes it, my lady? Will he be all right?"

Darcy straightened and sighed. "As I've already told you, Rory, he'll be fine if you let me get on and do what I need to. Now kindly shut the door and wait outside until I tell you."

"Aye. Sorry," Rory muttered. He darted back outside and closed the door behind him.

Darcy bent to her work. She soon had the wound nicely stitched and then gave the dog an injection to reverse the anesthetic. In only moments his tail was thumping against the table and he sat up, looking around groggily. Darcy scratched him behind the ears.

"No more chasing wild boar, you hear? Rory! You can come in now."

The kennel master's eyes widened as he saw the dog sitting there, happily nuzzling Darcy's hand.

"Yer a marvel, my lady," he said. "How can I ever thank ye?"

Darcy had begun to replace some of her supplies with local alternatives - antiseptic, bandages, needles and thread. So far it was working out well. She hoped to be able to replicate some of the drugs she used eventually, albeit in a rudimentary fashion.

"No need for thanks, Rory," she replied. "I'm just doing my job. Keep him confined to the kennels the next few days and make sure he doesn't put too much pressure on that wound. If he tries to lick it or damages his stitches bring him back and I'll make some sort of collar to stop him reaching the wound."

"Aye, I will." Rory picked up the hound and carried him out.

Darcy shut the door behind him and wiped her brow. She took off her apron, tossed it in the basket ready for laundry, did the same with her gloves, and then began scrubbing down the table. Thoughts of Quinn filled her mind. Where was he now? What was he doing? Was he safe?

Something boomed outside. A moment later it came again. And again. The warning drum? The door opened and Lily stuck her head in. She'd gone pale.

"What is it?" Darcy asked.

"Warning from the castle!" Lily cried. "We're under attack!"

With heart hammering Darcy followed Lily outside. All was chaos. The villagers were loading their things into barrows, onto their backs, into their arms, and hurrying towards the causeway and the safety of the castle.

"What's going on?" Darcy asked a teenage lad who dashed past leading two goats.

"The Murrays!" The lad replied, his voice shrill with fear. "They're coming!"

Darcy craned her neck to see and felt her blood go cold. A huge group of men was spilling over the brow of the hill, all mounted on warhorses, all heavily armed.

"Come on!" Lily cried, tugging on Darcy's arm. "We have to get to the castle!"

Together they joined the flow of frightened people heading towards the causeway. Darcy didn't understand how this could have happened. How had they evaded Quinn and his warriors? The Murray army was supposed to be a day's ride to the south. She had no time to ponder the question as she and Lily soon found themselves fleeing across the causeway towards the open gates of Dunbreggan and safety.

"Lady Darcy!" A voice called.

Darcy turned her head to see Owen, the blacksmith struggling towards her along the causeway. He was laden down with possessions and had his family around him, little Martha clinging to him with silent tears streaming down her face. Owen's eyes were wide with worry.

"Have you seen William, Lady Darcy?" he asked anxiously. "He said he had to go collect something and then dashed off before I could grab him. Nobody's seen him since."

Darcy laid a hand on the blacksmith's arm. Lily took the hands of the two youngest girls and made comforting noises as they clung to her skirts.

"His cat," Darcy said, clicking her fingers. "I'll bet he's gone back for his cat and her kittens."

"Curse the boy!" His father muttered. "Does he not ken that the wee cat has more chance of escaping these attackers than we do? That boy will be the death of me!"

Darcy sucked in a breath. Then she turned to face Lily and said in as calm a voice as she could manage. "Take Owen and the children to the castle. Rebecca will find a place for everyone. I'll go and find William."

Before she could change her mind, she spun and raced back along the causeway and into the village.

The attackers had almost reached the first of the buildings. She gritted her teeth, steeled her courage and ran. She skidded into the village square, deserted now, and turned left, pelting between the houses towards the blacksmith's forge. She daren't call William's name for fear of alerting the attackers so instead she looked around as she ran, scanning for any sign of the young boy.

She reached the blacksmith's house but found it empty. Cursing under her breath she sped around to the corner of the forge where she'd come to inspect the kittens. Sure enough William was crouched in the corner, the kittens - who were more like small cats now - in a box pressed against his chest protectively.

He looked up, terrified, as Darcy burst into the hut.

"William!" Darcy cried. "What are you doing? Your da is going out of his mind with worry!"

William threw himself at Darcy and wrapped one arm around her legs, the other cradling the kittens against his chest. They wriggled and mewed in distress.

"I had to come back for Tabs!" he cried. "But I canna find her and there's only the kittens here!" He sounded on the verge of tears.

Darcy crouched and gently brushed the hair from his eyes. She smiled at him. "Your cat is a sensible one. She'll have found a place to hide and will be back when it's safe. Trust me, William, she'll be fine." She ruffled his hair. "Now, how about we get you and those kittens to your father?"

She straightened and held out her hand which William gladly took. "We need to move quickly and quietly. Can you do that for me? If I tell you to stop, stop. If I tell you to run, run. Okay?"

William nodded and together they crept out of the hut, pausing only long enough for Darcy to check the coast was clear before hurrying away.

The attackers had entered the village. She heard them ransacking houses and calling to each other in hard voices. She gritted her teeth and kept moving, darting from house to house and keeping to the shadows as much as possible. They reached the village square and paused against the wall of the baker's shop, crouching behind some water barrels.

Carefully, Darcy looked out. Beyond the village square she could see the beginning of the causeway. The attackers hadn't got that far yet. If she and William could just reach that causeway before the attackers, they could reach Dunbreggan and safety. But the voices of the attackers were getting ever closer. If they were going to run for it they had to go now. But at that moment a voice spoke from the square.

"Come out, whoever ye are hiding behind those barrels. Don't make me come over there."

Darcy peered between a gap in the barrels to see a tall man standing in the middle of the square. The colors in his plaid marked him as a member of the Murray clan and he held a large sword in one hand. Darcy assessed her options. They didn't look good.

She turned to William. "Listen, to me," she whispered. "I'm going to stand up now and walk into that square. Don't follow me. I'll distract that man. When he turns his back, you run to the causeway. Run as fast as you can and don't look back. Okay?"

William's eyes were round with fear. "What about ye?"

"I'll be right behind you. Ready?"

He nodded. Darcy ruffled his hair and then stood up from behind the barrels, holding out her hands to show she carried no weapons.

"I'm here. I'm alone," she said to the man. She took a few paces into the square.

The man grinned. He looked to be in his middle years and sported a shaggy black beard and scarred arms as though he'd been in many fights. This didn't fill Darcy with confidence.

"Look what we have here," he said. "Dinna ye want to flee with the rest of yer kin, lass? Mayhap yer looking to find yerself a Murray warrior to keep ye warm, eh?"

She lifted her chin. "I was led to believe the Murray warriors were honorable. I gave myself up willingly and hope you will prove me right."

The man frowned but to Darcy's relief he sheathed his sword. Behind her, Darcy heard William shift and prayed silently that he wouldn't bolt too soon. Darcy stepped closer to the man and then took several steps to the left. As she'd hoped, he turned to follow her and now had his back to the water barrels. From the corner of her eye she saw William peek out from his hiding place. She had to keep the man distracted while William got away.

"Why are you here?" she asked. "Why have you brought armed men to a peaceful settlement?"

The man snorted. "Peaceful? Since when have the MacFarlanes been peaceful? Ye raid our lands at every opportunity. Ye sabotage our trade routes whenever ye get the chance. And now ye've gathered an army to invade our territory."

What on earth was he talking about? The MacFarlane clan had done no such thing. It was the Murrays who were the aggressors. However, she knew arguing with him would do no good.

"So what do you hope to achieve by coming here? This kind of attack on the MacFarlanes will only invite retaliation."

"Is that so?" he growled. "Mayhap we see things a little differently. Mayhap we see this as a chance to end the feud once and for all. When we take Dunbreggan the MacFarlanes will have nae choice but to come to terms with us. Terms of the Murray clan's choosing."

His attention was fixed wholly on her now. William took his chance. He shot out from behind the barrels, the box full of kittens still clutched his chest. The warrior turned in surprise but when he saw it was just a child he didn't bother to give chase. To Darcy's immense relief, William reached the causeway, pelted along it and into the safety of Dunbreggan.

"What have you found, Angus?" a voice said.

A group of mounted men trotted into the village square. Their horses sported fine trappings and the quality of the men's clothing marked them out as nobility. The man who'd spoken rode a beautiful white mare and wore a black velvet outfit with some kind of insignia worked on the arm in gold thread. The man had short, iron gray hair and a hard face that was all planes and angles. Cold blue eyes fixed on Darcy.

"One of the MacFarlane women, my lord," Angus replied, sheathing his sword. "She and her boy were hiding behind them barrels. The boy got away but maybe her husband will pay a ransom to get the wench back."

"Oh, I think he'll do much more than that," the newcomer said. He didn't sound like Quinn and the others. He had a refined English accent instead.

The man nudged his horse towards her and Darcy forced herself not to flinch as he approached. He reached down and lifted the chain around Darcy's neck, looking at the ring that hung there.

He pulled in a sharp breath. "Angus, you are to be commended. I think you've netted us a fine prize."

Angus frowned. "What do ye mean, my lord?"

"This isn't some woman of the MacFarlane clan. I recognize your description - and I'd recognize that ring anywhere. After all, I did kill its one-time owner.'"

Darcy gasped in sudden realization. "You're John de Clare."

He nodded. "And you're Quinn MacFarlane's woman." It wasn't a question. "I've heard tell of you. Some foreign woman who's finally captured the notorious bachelor's heart. It was foolish of him to give you his brother's ring but then Quinn MacFarlane has ever been foolish. Foolish to cross me. Foolish to think that he could escape my anger."

He let the ring drop and turned back to his men. "Angus, Roger, with me. The rest of you, scour the village for any other MacFarlanes that might be hiding."

Darcy swallowed. "What are you going to do with me?"

John de Clare flashed her a smile that had no mirth in it. "Oh, you're too precious a prize to risk in a siege. My army will take the castle. But you, my dear, are coming with me."

Chapter 17

Quinn realized he was holding the reins in a death grip and forced himself to relax. He rode by Robert's side at the head of the MacFarlane army, the double column of men streaming out behind them, so long that its end disappeared into the distance.

They'd traveled south-east all yesterday and this morning, sometimes at a trot, sometimes at a walk to let the horses rest, but always moving, desperate to reach the Point before the Murray army did. Now they were nearing their destination Quinn was filled with both apprehension and excitement.

Finally, it would be over. One way or another.

Robert held up a hand, giving the signal for the column to halt. Behind him the men pulled their horses up in a jingle of tack and the creaking of saddles. Together, Robert, Quinn, Fraser and Dougal dismounted and crept towards the edge of the ridge, being careful to keep low so they weren't outlined against the sky. Beyond lay the Point and slightly further east, Oldwyn's Barrow.

Somewhere between the two, they would find the Murray army.

They edged forward in silence and looked out over the landscape.

It was empty.

Oldwyn's Barrow rose out of the landscape, long and wide like some giant's grave. Quinn had expected to see the top bristling with warriors but the only creatures that moved there were a family of squabbling ravens. His eyes scanned the area, searching for any sign of the Murray forces. From this vantage point he could see for miles in all directions. The only things that met his eye were the purple heather covered hills of the Highlands.

"What is this?" Quinn barked. "Where are they?"

"Maybe they aren't traveling as fast as we thought," Fraser said.

But Robert was shaking his head, his face grave. "No. They're not coming."

He rose from the grass and began striding back towards the column. Quinn, Fraser and Dougal scrambled after him.

"What do ye mean, brother?" Quinn asked. "Our scouts-"

"Were tricked!" Robert cried, rounding on Quinn. "They were fed exactly the information John de Clare wanted us to know. He let our spies overhear just the right conversations, observe just the right movement of warriors. We've underestimated him. Again. My suspicions began when we came upon no tracks, no scouts, no signs of riders watching our approach. This only confirms them."

Quinn shook his head. "I dinna understand. Ye cannot fake the mobilization of an army. So the Murrays are out there somewhere. It they aren't marching to meet us then where are they?" But even as he asked the question a terrible realization crept up on him and his blood went cold. "Dunbreggan?"

Robert slowly nodded. "I fear this was a trap designed to pull our forces away from the castle so they can attack. It's a trap we walked right into."

Quinn was running before he knew it. He sprinted back to where they'd left the mounts, vaulted into the saddle and began bellowing orders. "We ride for Dunbreggan! We ride as though we have the devil on our tails and be prepared for a fight at the other end. De Clare is attacking our home! We're going to finish the bastard once and for all!"

The men were well trained and despite this sudden change in plan, they raised their weapons in salute. Robert and the others swung into their saddles. Robert nodded once at Quinn and then dug his heels into the flanks of his horse.

"Yah!"

The horse sprang away and Quinn nudged Silver after. Together the two brothers galloped for home, jumping ditches, thundering up hills and down them, sending birds bursting out of cover and flocks of sheep scattering from the path. Behind them rode their men, the orderly column breaking down until they became a horde that swept across the Highlands, weapons glinting in the sunlight.

Quinn felt as though a fire had been lit in his soul. They had to get back to Dunbreggan. His life, his very soul depended on it. If anything should happen to Darcy...

The ride back passed in a blur. The horses were soon lathered but they didn't dare stop to rest them. Each moment wasted gave the Murrays more time to launch their assault on the castle. They galloped for hours, desperately retracing the ground they covered yesterday, driving the horses to the brink of exhaustion. Finally, they reached the hills above Dunbreggan and Robert gave the instruction for them to slow the horses into a trot.

As they topped the rise and looked down on the castle, Quinn's heart jumped into his mouth. A black tide of men surrounded the castle. The causeway seethed with them and even more were flooded out around the causeway's mouth. The gates of the castle stood closed but even as he watched a dull boom echoed over the water as a battering ram smashed into them.

They didn't have much time. Once the gates were breached, it was all over.

Robert stood in his stirrups and turned to face his men. "We've trained for this!" he bellowed. "Each of ye knows yer place! Yer duty! We go to raise the siege of Dunbreggan! Of our home! We will not rest until the invaders are driven off! Until our home, our loved ones are safe!" He drew his sword and held it high above him. It glinted bright silver in the afternoon sun. "For Dunbreggan and Clan MacFarlane!"

"Dunbreggan and MacFarlane!" The men bellowed in response.

Robert pulled hard on the reins, causing his mount to rear, hooves pawing the air, and then he went thundering down the hill towards the waiting horde. Feeling the thrill of battle beginning to bubble inside him, Quinn set his heels to his horse's flanks and went speeding after his brother. His lips pulled back to bare his teeth in a snarl. The muscles in his arms and legs tensed, ready for action.

The Murrays saw them coming, of course. They were well versed in the arts of battle and had posted scouts to keep watch for any sign of the returning MacFarlanes. The only consolation in all of this was that the Murrays couldn't have known that they'd traveled to Oldwyn's Barrow so quickly and therefore discovered the ruse much sooner than the Murrays would have hoped.

Even so, the Murray forces turned with practiced ease, splitting so that one half still laid siege to the castle while the other turned to face the threat streaming down at them from the hillside. Most of the Murray forces were infantry and under usual circumstances cavalry would sweep them away easily. But amongst the winding streets of the village, the MacFarlane heavy horse would bring no advantage.

The Murray forces formed a pike wall and turned to defend the entrance to the causeway. Iron tipped pikes, longer than a man, bristled in a thicket that would skewer any horse foolish enough to try to jump it. So, as Quinn, Robert and the others reached the line, they kicked their feet free of the stirrups and leapt from the saddle, hitting the ground in a roll and coming up with swords swinging.

The pike wall was too ungainly to bring the weapons to bear quickly against the MacFarlane warriors. Quinn swung his sword, cutting cleanly through a row of three pikes and slammed into a warrior, knocking him to the ground and moving on to the man behind.

The Murray line buckled under the MacFarlane onslaught. All around him Quinn heard the clang and clamor of battle. The shouting of men, the clash of weapons, the tramp of feet, but he didn't dare spare a glance for his comrades. All his attention was focused on the foes in front of him.

Realizing their pike wall had failed, the Murrays threw down the ungainly weapons and drew their swords instead. Quinn ducked under the swinging blade of a shaven-headed warrior and then caught the next downswing on his own sword with a clang of metal. Pivoting to his left, he brought his sword around in an arc and ran the man through. He yanked his sword from the man's body as he fell and spun to meet his next opponent.

Quinn's world shrank to the tiny space around him in which he fought. He kicked, punched, parried with his blade and cut down any who stood in his way. A thought kept going round and round in his head, driving him on.

Must reach the gates. Must reach the gates.

Soon his lungs were burning and sweat was dripping down his forehead into his eyes. He dashed it away angrily and looked around for his next opponent. All around him Murray warriors lay groaning on the ground. Some would never rise again and Quinn was sorry for that but they knew what the price might be when they rode against Dunbreggan. A space had cleared around him and he took the time to get his bearings.

He'd managed to fight his way through the line of Murray warriors and was halfway along the causeway. And he was alone. He'd fought clear of his comrades who were engaged in battles of their own further back. Ahead of him was a line of hostile warriors with weapons bristling.

The end of the causeway was in sight and through the besiegers Quinn could see the gates of Dunbreggan. Thankfully, they still held although that wouldn't be the case for much longer if they didn't stop that battering ram.

Quinn raised his sword over his head and bellowed at the top of his voice, "To me! Warriors of MacFarlane, to me!"

With a roar they answered him. Robert, Fraser and two dozen others dispatched their opponents and surged towards him. Quinn felt carried up on their battle cry and he turned, howling his fury, and led his men, his brother at his side, to crash in to the Murray lines that were assaulting the gates of their home.

Quinn fought with redoubled fury. *Must reach the gates,* his thoughts went round and round. He looked intently at the face of each man he fought, hoping to come across John de Clare but he didn't see him anywhere.

"Where is yer leader?" he shouted at a Murray warrior as they traded sword blows. "Where is John de Clare?"

The man didn't bother to answer. His attention was focused on deflecting Quinn's attack. Quinn dropped to the ground, spun with one leg out, and took the warrior's legs out from under him. Then he dispatched him with a quick thrust to the gut.

"Where is John de Clare?" he bellowed at the next man.

"How should I know?" The man grunted. "I'm the man's warrior, not his nursemaid!"

"Quinn!" bellowed Robert. "The gates!"

The battering ram thudded into the gates with an ear shattering boom. To Quinn's horror the gates split, sending splinters of wood showering over the attackers.

But if the attackers thought that breaking the gates meant taking the castle, they were in for a surprise. The garrison that Robert had left to defend Dunbreggan poured out of the breach, weapons swinging. A melee erupted, fierce close-quarter fighting that left no room for mercy.

"To the gates!" Quinn bellowed. "Don't let them get inside the bailey!"

His men redoubled their efforts and fought furiously. At last they reached the end of the causeway and threw themselves into the fierce fighting in front of the gates. Quinn lost all track of time. His world became one of screaming muscles, glittering blades, the stink of sweat and the clash of weapons.

But then suddenly, finally, there were no more enemies to fight. Quinn found himself face-to-face with the defenders right outside the breached gates. In a daze, he stumbled to a halt and turned. The Murray warriors were fleeing along the causeway and back up into the hills. The MacFarlane warriors jumped onto their mounts to harry them as they fled and ensure they left MacFarlane lands.

Panting, Quinn leaned on his sword. Robert staggered up, looking as exhausted as Quinn felt, followed by Fraser and then Dougal.

"Well met, my lord," said Cameron, the captain of the castle garrison. He sported a cut along his forehead but seemed otherwise unharmed. "They came without warning but we managed to get the villagers inside the castle before they arrived. Thank the Lord ye arrived before they managed to breach the gates."

Robert clapped the man on the shoulder. "Thank the Lord indeed. And thank ye and yer men as well for yer quick thinking and bravery. We'll go to the main hall where we'll take tally of the casualties." He smiled wryly. "A cup or two of ale wouldn't go amiss either."

The ruined gates were opened and Robert led the way back into Dunbreggan. Quinn was exhausted. His limbs felt like they were made of lead. And yet, at the same time, excitement bubbled in his stomach. Darcy would be waiting for him. He couldn't wait to take her in his arms and then carry her up to their chamber and spend a good while showing her how much he'd missed her.

As Robert led the victorious warriors into the outer bailey a cheer went up. People thronged the courtyard and the battlements, all waving and calling out greetings to the returning warriors. Quinn's eyes scanned the crowd, searching for one face.

At the top of the steps leading to the keep stood Rebecca and Lily. Darcy wasn't with them. Where could she be? Probably tending to some sick animal knowing Darcy. Still, he would soon hold her in his arms and everything would be all right.

He, Robert and Fraser made their way up the steps. Rebecca threw her arms around her husband and Lily greeted her betrothed in a similar fashion. Then the two women turned to Quinn with a look on their faces that made the hairs stand up on the back of his neck.

"Quinn, I'm so sorry," Rebecca murmured, laying a hand on his arm.

"Sorry? For what?" He looked around again. "Where's Darcy?"

Rebecca shook her head. "They took her. De Clare took her."

Quinn's blood went cold. His heart was suddenly thundering against his ribs. It was all he could do to croak out, "Where? When?"

"Just before the siege began," Rebecca replied. "She went back to find William. The boy managed to escape but Darcy was captured. We don't know what's become of her. Quinn, I-"

Quinn didn't hear the rest of Rebecca's words. He was already sprinting back down the steps, bellowing for his horse. Robert and Fraser caught him before he'd even made it to the causeway. They ran beside him, keeping time with his urgent stride.

"Don't try and stop me, brother," Quinn growled at him. "I'll nae rest until I find her."

"I wasnae gonna try and stop ye, brother," Robert replied. He shared a look with Fraser. "We're coming with ye. De Clare must be made to pay for this."

Quinn met his brother's stern gaze and nodded. Together the three of them jogged back across the causeway to where their horses were being held by grooms. They swung into the saddle, spun their mounts and charged off.

Quinn could barely think for the blood roaring in his ears. If anything befell Darcy...

He wouldn't let it. She was his woman. His love. He would rescue her or die in the attempt. It was as simple as that.

Chapter 18

Darcy gritted her teeth as the motion of the trotting horse made her bounce around like a sack of potatoes. Her back ached and she was sure some of her teeth must be loose from the endless jolting.

John de Clare took no notice of her discomfort. She sat in the saddle in front of him, wrists tied, gripping the pommel for dear life. John de Clare himself was a cold, hard presence at her back. He didn't speak to her. In fact, the only time he opened his mouth was to bark orders at his men.

They'd ridden hastily south along the shores of the loch, and ironically along almost the same route that Darcy had taken when she had fled Dunbreggan. They'd encountered not a soul. All the crofters roundabout had been evacuated into the castle and Quinn's force was further east, riding for the spot where they believed the Murray army waited for them.

Which was a trick, of course.

Darcy's stomach turned over as she thought of Dunbreggan under siege. Was everyone safe? Had the gates held? How was Rebecca? Lily? William? If anything happened to them she didn't know what she would do.

And then there was Quinn. Her heart ached at the thought of him. She had to force herself not to keep glancing over her shoulder, hoping to spot him galloping after them.

Will I ever see him again? Darcy asked herself. She pressed her lips into a hard, flat line. *Of course I will!* She told herself savagely. *I'll get out of this somehow and find my way back to him. Remember the brigands on the road? I got out of that all right didn't I? This will be no different.*

The thought steadied her a little and she forced herself to look around, trying to figure out where they might be headed. But the Highlands spread out around her, purple and green under the summer sun, and she could see no landmarks to speak of.

"Where are we going?" she asked John de Clare.

She'd asked this question countless times and he'd ignored her each time so she was surprised when he said, "My stronghold, of course."

"You realize Quinn and Robert will be coming after us you don't you?"

"Oh, I'll be counting on it."

The coldness in his voice made her shiver. "Why? What have you gained from any of this?"

His hand tightened on the reins. "Vengeance. The MacFarlanes took everything from me. Because of them I was left a destitute beggar, stripped of all but my name. I've worked for years to repair the damage they did to me. And my resurrection will be complete when I drive my sword through Robert and Quinn MacFarlane's hearts."

A shot of fear went through Darcy. The man talked about killing Quinn and Robert as easily as if he was discussing the weather.

"You killed their elder brother," she said. "Isn't that vengeance enough?"

"Enough?" he barked. "It will never be enough! Quinn MacFarlane escaped me that day. He won't escape again."

"And then what?" She forced herself to ask. "Say you do manage to take vengeance on the MacFarlane brothers? You think it will end there? The feud between the Murrays and the MacFarlanes will only escalate. Their people die. Your people will die. How can that benefit anyone?"

"Enough talking!" he snapped.

He kicked his horse into a canter and Darcy was forced to cling onto the saddle pommel even harder lest she lose her seating and go crashing to the ground.

The loch shone off to her left, glimmering silver in the sunlight. Darcy found herself gazing at it, almost mesmerized. Then something caught her eye. There was a reflection in the water. The reflection of a tall creature. Darcy's head whipped around and there, sure enough, a red deer was stood on an outcrop of rock, watching them pass. She didn't seem afraid of this group of armed men passing so close below. Her liquid eyes tracked them as they moved and Darcy could have sworn her eyes were fixed on Darcy herself.

"Did you see that?" Darcy asked.

"I saw nothing," John de Clare growled. "And I said no more talking!"

Darcy craned her head to look over de Clare's shoulder. She could make out the rocky outcrop but nothing stood there now. She shook her head. It hadn't been her imagination, she was sure of it. It was a red deer with a white stripe down its nose.

Just like the one she'd followed through the stone arch and back in time five hundred years.

Despite the long ride John de Clare and his men didn't stop to rest. Darcy's body felt like one long ache and her throat was parched. Despite this, she started to drowse in the saddle. She was jolted out of her stupor by a sudden cry.

"What's that?"

Her eyes flew open to see one of the men pulling his horse roughly to the right, out of the way of the creature standing calmly in their path.

The red deer.

It stood there, nose twitching as it watched them, large eyes scanning the group. Then it turned and bounded away.

One of the men untied his bow from his saddle and looked around eagerly.

John de Clare scowled at the man. "We don't have the time to go hunting, you fool! Put the bow away!"

The man frowned at his leader but did as he was bid without argument. De Clare gave the signal and they broke into a canter once more. Darcy was beginning to lose hope of Quinn catching them before they crossed into Murray lands. De Clare was relentless and they traveled swiftly, and with a head start. Even if Quinn was following, even if he was driving his horse to exhaustion, he still wouldn't be able to catch them.

Don't think like that, Darcy told herself. *Quinn will come. He will.*

"Look!"

One of the men was pointing towards the loch. A white mist was rising from the water. It rose like steam from a bubbling kettle and coalesced to form a thick white blanket hanging low over the surface. Then, as Darcy watched in fascination, the fog began to move. The breeze blew it inland towards Darcy and de Clare. The fog spilled over the shore of the loch and up over the surrounding heathland.

Wispy white tendrils touched Darcy's skin and hair, leaving tiny droplets of water behind. In only moments the Highlands and even the loch itself had disappeared, enveloped in whiteness. Around her, de Clare's men became indistinct shadows.

"What is this?" De Clare growled. "Sea fog on a loch? I've never heard the like." He scanned around, searching for his men. "All of you, in a line! Stay close! If anyone gets lost I'm not coming back to find you!"

"We can't keep moving in this!" one of his men replied. "We could easily lose our way, get turned around and end up going back the way we came!"

"Or worse," another man called. "We might tumble down one of the hills and into the loch. I canna swim!"

"We keep moving!" De Clare bellowed. "You'll do as you're ordered, damn you!"

Grumbling under their breath, the men did as they were told. They formed a line, each rider moving in single file with the nose of each horse to the rump of the one in front. They moved at a snail's pace. Any faster and they risked losing each other in the thick white fog.

Darcy's mind raced. Could she somehow use this to her advantage? Could she slip from the saddle and run? Would she be able to lose herself in the fog and find a hiding place where John de Clare wouldn't find her?

"Don't get any ideas, girl," he growled in her ear. "Any hint of disobedience from you and I'll tie you up and sling you across the back of my horse. Clear?"

"Clear," Darcy said through gritted teeth.

So much for a chance at escape. De Clare would be watching her even closer from now on.

Please hurry, Quinn, Darcy thought desperately. *Because this advantage won't last forever.*

Quinn rode like a man possessed. John de Clare had made no effort to hide his trail. He wanted Quinn to follow. Quinn knew very well that this was a trap he was riding straight into. He didn't care. The only thing that mattered was getting Darcy back safely.

The thought of her in danger made his stomach clench with fear. If de Clare harmed her...

He gritted his teeth, pushing that thought away. Mud flew from beneath his horse's hooves as he thundered down a rise, Robert and Fraser close behind.

He had to catch up with de Clare before he passed into Murray territory. If he did that de Clare would have the full backing of Murray forces and Quinn would find himself trying to orchestrate a rescue in hostile lands.

But he was beginning to despair of catching them in time. De Clare had a significant head start and from the width of the horses' hoof prints Quinn could tell that they were moving very quickly indeed. De Clare wouldn't care if he killed the horses in his mad dash to safety. Just as long as he got home with his prize that was all that would matter to that snake of a man.

"Brother!" Robert called. "Watch out!"

Quinn looked up to see a deer standing directly in the path of his horse. It didn't bolt as he approached, just stood there calmly watching him. With a cry, Quinn yanked at the reins, sending his horse veering off to the left, avoiding the beast. As he thundered past, Quinn glanced over his shoulder and realized that not only had the deer not ran from the men, but that it was now shadowing them, matching their pace easily just a few paces to the left.

The hairs rose on the back of Quinn's neck. Thoughts of Irene MacAskill entered unbidden into his mind. He'd been thinking of the strange old woman more and more lately.

What do ye want, Quinn? She had asked him. He'd been unable to answer at the time. Now, if she asked the question again, his answer would be easy. *I want Darcy. I want a simple life with a wife and bairns.*

"What's that up ahead?" called Fraser suddenly.

He was pointing to the loch. Several leagues away to the south, a mist had gathered above the water. It boiled up from the loch and covered the shore and the hills beyond. It was many miles away yet but if it didn't dissipate soon they'd be forced to ride through it.

"Would ye look at that?" shouted Fraser. "I've never seen the like! It'll make riding pretty damned difficult!"

"Aye, it will," Quinn agreed. "For de Clare as well as for us. Unless I miss my guess, the head start de Clare had would put him right about where that fog has developed."

Robert stood in his stirrups, eyes narrowed as he peered ahead. "I believe yer right, brother. This might be just the piece of luck we need if we're to catch these bastards before they cross the border."

Quinn nodded and nudged his horse to greater speed.

"How long do we go on like this?" one of the men grumbled.

"You want to stop?" de Clare growled. "You scared of a little fog? You're a disgrace to the Murray clan! Shut your mouth and keep riding unless you want to taste steel!"

The man licked his lips. "Nae, lord. I was just saying-"

"It's not your job to say anything! It's your job to follow my orders!"

Darcy kept her eyes fixed straight ahead even though through the swirling mists she could see nothing. At least this way she could kind of pretend that she was alone rather than riding with John de Clare, Quinn's most hated enemy.

She could well understand how he'd climbed to power. The man could be charismatic when he needed to be and downright terrifying as well. He had that same knack of calm authority that Quinn had. But where Quinn's authority was tempered with kindness and compassion, she saw none of that in John de Clare. She saw only ruthlessness, a man who would do anything to get what he wanted. She wasn't ashamed to admit that he frightened her.

She spotted something in the fog ahead. "What was that?"

John de Clare's head whipped round. "What was what?"

"I thought I saw something." She leaned low over the horse's neck, squinting into the distance. "The fog is thinning. Look."

Sure enough, the thick blanket of white began to grow thinner and the surrounding landscape appeared out of the murk. Suddenly Darcy found herself under a bright blue sky with the sun blazing overhead.

John de Clare pulled his horse to a halt. Darcy took the opportunity to look around. She had no idea how far they'd traveled in the fog. The loch still lay to their left but it was wider here, so wide that Darcy could hardly make out the other side. The loch shore had become a sandy beach.

Then she spotted something and Darcy's stomach flipped over. There, just a few meters to her left on the loch shore, rose the very thing she'd been trying unsuccessfully to find all this time.

The stone arch.

It rose gracefully into the air, one side attached to a sheer cliff, the other arcing out over the shore to come down into the cold waters of the loch itself.

Darcy's pulse quickened. She glanced at the men around her but they didn't take any notice. They were busy checking their horses and figuring out exactly where they were.

John de Clare yanked his horse around to face the way they'd come. He reached into his saddlebags and took out a long leather tube with lenses fixed in either end. He pressed the tube against his eye and scanned their trail.

"Curse it!" he growled. "They're coming."

Darcy's heart thudded. Quinn! It must be Quinn!

"So?" one of the men said. "We wanted him to follow us dinna we? We just keep riding and draw him into the trap we're going to set."

With a sneer John de Clare flung the eyeglass at the man. "Idiot! Any advantage we had we lost in that damned fog. If I was a superstitious man I'd say it was sent to thwart us! Look for yourself. They'll be on us before we can reach the castle. We'll make our stand here - on ground of our choosing. We outnumber them and we have an ace up our sleeve."

He swung out of the saddle and then pulled Darcy roughly to the ground beside him. After so long in the saddle Darcy's legs were weak and she would have fallen on her backside had de Clare not kept a tight grip on her arm.

"Let me go!" she cried. "Let me go and Quinn might leave you alive!"

If she thought her bravado would intimidate John de Clare, she was disappointed. He just watched her impassively. The expression on his face made her shiver. There was nothing in his eyes. No emotion at all. She'd expected to see anger, rage, the burning need for vengeance. But there was nothing. That scared her more than his fury would have done.

"I admire your optimism," he said. "But I'm afraid it's misplaced. Quinn will be the one who won't leave here alive."

"You really believe you can beat Quinn in battle?" Darcy said. "He'll kick your ass! He's the best warrior in the MacFarlane clan! You won't know what hit you!"

"Who said anything about battle? You seem to be laboring under the delusion that I plan to meet Quinn in combat. That is not the plan and never has been. When I attacked Dunbreggan I planned to capture Lady Rebecca. But instead I captured you and I've come to realize that you're an even greater prize. Quinn is an honorable fool. He'll do anything to save his betrothed's life." This time Darcy did see something in John de Clare's eyes. They gleamed with an almost savage glee. "Even give up his own life."

Darcy went cold. "What do you mean?"

De Clare moved like lightning. One minute he was stood in front of her, the next he was behind her, one arm across her throat, the other pressing the tip of a dagger against her chest.

"I mean, my dear," he said into her ear. "That when Quinn arrives I'll offer him a deal. None of his men need to die here today. They can all walk away, go back to Dunbreggan and their families. They can even take you with them. All Quinn has to do is stand there whilst I stab my sword into his treacherous heart. If he doesn't agree I can find other places to put my blade."

He increased the pressure on the dagger and Darcy gasped as she felt it bite her skin. A thin rivulet of blood stained her chest.

"You understand my meaning?" he asked.

"I understand," Darcy said. "You're going to hold me hostage and use me against Quinn. That's a coward's way of doing things. Don't you have any honor?"

He barked a bitter laugh. "Honor? Honor is an indulgence. I'd rather have vengeance. And soon, my dear, you will help me get it."

He pushed her roughly away from him and she staggered and fell to her knees in the heather.

De Clare's men had arranged themselves across the hilltop in a formation that would give them the high ground and force Quinn and the others to fight uphill. Darcy was no warrior but even she understood that this would put them at a disadvantage.

Don't come here, Quinn, she thought to herself. *It's a trap. Please don't come here.*

But she knew he would. De Clare's plan was brilliant in its simplicity. Quinn would do it. He would give up his life for hers. She would be forced to watch him die.

I can't do that, she thought. *I won't. I won't allow it to come to this.*

She glanced around. The stone arch lay so close. Tiny veins in the rock caught the light and made it glitter. If she could reach it then maybe she could escape this predicament and save Quinn from this trap. De Clare couldn't user her against him if the archway sent her home.

She watched John de Clare, timing her moment. He bent to check the stirrups on his saddle, his horse momentarily blocking his view of her.

Darcy seized her chance.

She sprang to her feet and bolted towards the loch shore. It was difficult to run with her hands bound and the hillocky tufts of heather threatened to trip her. Nonetheless, she ran with all the speed she could muster, throwing herself in a slide down the sandy bank and onto the beach.

Her feet hit the sand and she took off along the shore. Her breath burned in her chest and her heart thumped but she carried on running, not daring to look behind her.

The stone arch loomed ahead - and there was somebody standing in front of it.

With a yelp of surprise, Darcy skidded to a halt. Her eyes widened as she recognized the short, round woman who stood there as if waiting for Darcy.

Irene MacAskill.

She wore a long flowing dress of sixteenth century cut rather than the smart business suit Darcy had last seen her in, but Darcy would recognize her anywhere. That impish smile, those rosy cheeks, those large brown eyes that seemed to look right into Darcy's soul. The silver deer brooch was pinned to her dress.

"Well, it's about time, lassie," Irene said in her singsong voice.

"What...what are you doing here?" Darcy panted.

"Waiting for ye, of course, dearie," Irene said, cocking her head. "Waiting to discover what choice ye'll make. It's all about choices in the end, ye see."

"You came through the arch?" Darcy asked. "You came back in time just like I did?"

"Nae, lassie. I dinna need the arch to do that. I'm of this time and yer time and all the times between."

Her words made no sense but Darcy didn't have time to figure it out. "If I go through the arch now, will it take me home? Will it save Quinn from John de Clare's trap?"

"Aye, it will. De Clare canna follow ye. If ye return home, he canna use ye against Quinn. Quinn will be free to fight."

Darcy paused. If she went through that archway, all this would be over. She'd be back in her own time, in her own place.

But without Quinn.

Yet what choice did she have? De Clare and his men would be coming for her. They'd use her against Quinn. They'd hold her hostage until he did what they wanted. She had to go through the arch. It was the only way to keep him safe.

"Not easy, is it, lassie?" Irene MacAskill asked. "The best choices never are. Ye have one to make now, lassie. Quinn MacFarlane is up there fighting for ye. I have to admit he passed his test better than I ever would have hoped. How will ye face yers? Will ye go home to yer old life or will ye walk back up that hill and fight for the man ye love?"

Up ahead the fog was clearing. One minute the landscape was obscured by a white blanket, the next that white blanket broke apart to reveal a group of mounted men waiting for them on the hilltop.

"That's them!" shouted Quinn, standing in his stirrups as he galloped. "Fraser, cut round to the left and stop them flanking us! Robert, go right. I'll take center."

His companions nodded grimly. They were outnumbered by de Clare and his men. Usually, not good odds.

But not today, Quinn thought. *The odds don't matter. We will prevail. We have to.*

The men atop the hillside sat their mounts calmly and waited. Quinn's eyes scanned the group, searching for Darcy and John de Clare. He saw neither of them.

He drew his sword and held it over his head. "For MacFarlane!"

With a roar, de Clare's men spurred their mounts into motion. Quinn smashed into the nearest rider with enough force to almost rip him from the saddle. He clung on, spinning his mount and swinging his blade at de Clare's man. They exchanged blows in quick succession, the sound of clanging metal echoing across the hilltop. The man was good, obviously an accomplished swordsman.

But he wasn't good enough. Quinn feinted to his left, drawing the man after him and then pulled his mount in a tight circle and swung his blade to strike with the flat of the blade against the man's temple. The man's eyes rolled back in his head and he toppled from his horse.

Quinn's companions were involved in fierce close-quarter fighting. Robert was hemmed in by two of de Clare's men. But Robert was an expert horseman and his mount danced nimbly in and out, turning almost on a sixpence so that by the time the two men got their weapons to bear, he'd already switched positions. The two men hampered each other, seemingly unable to coordinate their attack. As Quinn watched, Robert ran one through and then barged the other's mount, knocking him to the ground.

Quinn looked around desperately, searching for some sign of Darcy and John de Clare. Where were they? Why wasn't she here?

Turning his mount in a circle, he caught a glimpse of John de Clare scrambling down the hill on foot, towards the loch shore. With a cry, he spurred his horse into motion, driving his mount to the edge of the hill and then springing from the saddle. He slid and scrambled down the slope until he reached the shore of the loch.

He flicked a stray strand of hair from his face irritably and looked around, sword clutched in one hand. Perhaps fifty paces ahead of him an archway stretched from the hillside into the loch. To his immense relief he saw Darcy standing in front of that archway.

But pelting towards her across the shore was John de Clare.

Fury bloomed in Quinn's chest. He took off after de Clare, his feet pounding the ground, his arms pumping. He would not let de Clare reach Darcy.

"Turn and face me!" Quinn yelled. "Turn and face me like a man, coward!"

Quinn was gaining on de Clare. When he was perhaps five paces behind the man, Quinn bunched his muscles and launched himself through the air. He collided with de Clare and sent them both sprawling to the ground.

De Clare's fist connected with Quinn's chin hard enough to snap his head to one side. Quinn rolled away just as de Clare's sword thudded into the sand where he'd lain.

"You bastard," de Clare growled. "I'll kill you."

Quinn staggered to his feet. He'd lost his sword when he threw himself at de Clare and it lay several feet behind his opponent, too far for him to recover. Quinn dropped into a fighting crouch, hands curled into fists, eyes fixed on his enemy.

De Clare had regained his feet and was standing with his sword tip resting in the sand, eyes glaring hatred at Quinn. Slowly, they began to circle. Quinn risked a glance at Darcy. She was watching the fight with wide, fearful eyes. And there was somebody else with her.

Irene MacAskill.

He didn't have time to ponder what the woman's presence might mean. All his attention was focused on John de Clare.

Without warning the man sprang at him. He moved like lightning. Quinn threw himself to his right, getting out of the way of de Clare's blade just in time. It scored a graze along his cheek rather than taking off his head.

Quinn spun and lashed out with his foot. His kick caught de Clare's knee and made him stagger, giving Quinn just enough time to roll and grab the hilt of his sword lying in the sand. He brought his blade up just in time to catch the downswing of de

Clare's two-handed stroke. The two blades met with an almighty clang.

Quinn heaved on his sword, pushing de Clare back long enough for him to regain his feet. De Clare came at him and they traded blows, swinging and ducking and parrying, each trying to get through the other's defense. De Clare was good. By God, he was good. His reputation as one of the best swordsman in the land was not exaggerated. In only seconds, Quinn found himself fighting for his life.

And still Darcy stood there, watching. And still Irene MacAskill stood by her side, watching.

Choices, she had once said to Quinn. It's always about choices. The question was now, what choice had she offered Darcy?

Why do ye stand there, love? Quinn thought. *Run. Run!*

Chapter 19

Darcy was frozen to the spot. She watched the fight with horror, fear running through her veins like acid.

John de Clare fought like a madman. Quinn was hard pressed to keep him at bay. The two men's swords were a blur, their movements quick as they tussled back and forth across the beach.

She had to do something. She had to help Quinn. But she couldn't move. She felt the pull of the stone arch behind her. She felt the pull of Quinn ahead of her. It was like being caught between two magnets.

Irene MacAskill cocked her head as she watched Darcy. The old woman was as eerily calm as ever, completely unperturbed by the fight going on just meters from where she stood.

"That's the pull of home, ye feel," she said. "It's a strong one isn't it? Now you have to make yer choice, lassie."

The murky blankness inside the stone arch suddenly shimmered. It coalesced into an image, an image of home. Darcy saw the city with its bustling streets, lines of traffic, coffee shops, shopping malls. It seemed so vibrant, so full of life. A pang of homesickness went through her, so strong it almost drove her to her knees.

All she had to do was step through the archway and she would be home.

All she had to do was abandon Quinn.

But she couldn't do it. She couldn't leave him. He needed her.

Quinn's attention, which should have been focused wholly on the man he fought, was divided. He kept glancing in Darcy's direction when he should've been watching his opponent. And each time he glanced at her, a look of worry and doubt flashed into his eyes as though he somehow knew she teetered on the edge of a decision that could take her away from him for ever.

She glanced over her shoulder at the image of home in the stone arch and then very deliberately turned her back on it.

What is home? she thought. *Home is the man I love. Home is Quinn.*

"Quinn!" she bellowed. "Fight! Beat him! I'm here! I love you!"

As if drawing strength from her words, Quinn redoubled his efforts. His blows became harder, quicker, his feet moved faster and a look of steely determination came over his face. He began pushing John de Clare back towards the water.

But John de Clare redoubled his efforts too. It was a stalemate. They were too evenly matched. Their blades locked together and the two men pushed against each other, their faces mere inches apart.

"Ye killed my brother!" Quinn snarled at de Clare. "I won't rest until ye've paid for yer crime!"

"He got what he deserved," de Clare spat back. "He ruined my life. I lost everything because of him, because of the MacFarlane clan! It's taken me years to rebuild all you took from me. I will have my vengeance!"

"And ye thought ye'd do that by attacking Dunbreggan? By hurting innocent people? Yer argument is with me and Robert, de Clare. Why should my clan pay for yer hatred?"

"Nobody is innocent," de Clare grated. "And when you're dead I'll kill your brother. Then I'll ride to Dunbreggan in victory as the conqueror of the MacFarlanes!"

"Yer a fool!" Quinn growled. "The siege has been raised! Dunbreggan is free. Ye've failed, de Clare."

De Clare's eyes widened and for a moment he seemed stunned by this news. But he mastered himself in an instant. "You think that matters? I command the Murray clan now. We are far stronger than you could ever hope to be. I'll take Dunbreggan one day. I'm a patient man, I know how to wait. Killing you today will be enough for now."

With that, he braced his feet and pushed with all his strength. Quinn took a grudging step backwards. De Clare lifted a foot and hooked it around Quinn's, tripping him. It was a dirty move and Quinn wasn't expecting it. With a curse he staggered back, sword flying from his hand.

With a shout of triumph de Clare swung his sword.

"Quinn!" Darcy screamed.

His eyes snapped to hers. His eyes were filled with love. He wasn't afraid. He seemed resigned as de Clare's blade swung at him.

Darcy felt something touch her palm. She looked down to see she was holding the wolf-head dagger Quinn had made her and the bonds tying her wrists had been cut. Where had the dagger come from? She glanced at Irene MacAskill who merely shrugged. She didn't stop to question.

"Catch!" Darcy screamed.

She flung the dagger towards Quinn. He caught it hilt-first and rammed it into de Clare's chest just as he began the killing blow. De Clare's eyes widened. He stared at the blade sticking from his chest. De Clare's mouth worked as if he was trying to form words but no sounds came out. Then he toppled backwards onto the beach and lay still.

"Quinn!"

Darcy scrambled across the sand and threw herself into his arms. He held her tight, pressing her against him, his strong arms around her.

"Hush, love," he whispered in her ear. "It's over. Yer safe now."

Darcy clung to him. She never wanted to let him go. He was her home. How could she have ever thought otherwise?

He pressed his forehead against hers. "Are ye all right, love? He dinna hurt ye?"

"No. I'm fine."

"I'm glad." He looked over her shoulder and tensed.

Darcy turned to see Irene MacAskill approaching. She smiled warmly at them.

"So it seems the choice has finally been made. I feel quite the proud mother hen."

"What are ye doing here, woman?" Quinn snapped. "I should have guessed ye'd have something to do with this mischief!"

"You two know each other?" Darcy asked, confused.

"Aye," Quinn said. "She did share my campfire one night. Told me I'd have choices to make, whatever that meant. Then she disappeared. It was shortly after that I met ye, love. The clan say she may be a witch."

Irene MacAskill raised an eyebrow and tutted at that. "And what do ye think, Quinn MacFarlane? Have I led ye astray? Have I done aught but bring ye yer heart's desire, just as I promised?"

Quinn frowned. "Aye, ye've done that, I canna deny. I ken it was ye who sent the fog to slow de Clare and gave Darcy the dagger to throw to me. I thank ye for that."

Darcy looked from Irene to Quinn and back again. "Choices? Heart's desire? You asked me the same thing. Only you asked me five hundred years away."

Quinn appeared startled at that. "What do ye mean, love?"

Irene MacAskill chuckled. "Ye've done it now, lass. Mayhap it's time for the truth."

Darcy swallowed. Where to begin? What to say? Quinn was watching her intently, a slightly puzzled expression on his handsome face. She sucked in a breath. Best to get it over with.

"I'm sorry, Quinn. I've not been completely honest with you. I'm not from some land over the ocean. Well, I am, but that's not the whole story. I'm from the future. Five hundred years in the future to be exact. I walked under that archway and was transported here. That's why I was desperate to find this place again - it was the only way I knew to get back to my own time."

Quinn stared at her as if she'd gone mad. "Yer from the future?"

Darcy nodded. "Yes. From the twenty-first century."

Quinn scrubbed a hand through his hair. "I knew there was something about ye, lass. Something more than just being from a different land. Yer words, yer ways. The way ye operated on Old Mac's ewe that time and the arcane equipment ye used - it gave me pause, I have to admit. And I should have guessed at something like this when one of the fae is involved." He fixed Irene MacAskill with a stern glare. "For that is what ye are, is it not?"

Irene MacAskill shrugged. "Of course. What else could I be? It's my duty to bring balance to the world. To bring together those halves that make a whole. Ye two are such, even though ye were born five hundred years apart. I gave ye the opportunity to meet yer destiny but it had to be yer choice. Now the choice has been made."

She turned and began walking away.

"Wait," Quinn called after her. "That's it? Yer just gonna walk away?"

"My job here is done," Irene said. "She chose ye, ye big oaf. And believe me, that couldnae have been an easy choice. The twenty-first century has many delights." She closed her eyes and said dreamily. "Chocolate. Cappuccino. Doughnuts." She opened her eyes, winked at them both, and walked off.

In the blink of an eye she was gone but Darcy thought she caught sight of a red deer bounding away across the hills.

Quinn let out a long sigh. He placed his hands on Darcy's shoulders and turned her to face him. "Ye have no idea how glad I am to see ye safe and well, love. I've never been more scared in my life than when I found out he'd taken ye."

Darcy blinked back tears. "Oh, Quinn." She put her arms around him and hugged him close.

"There ye are!"

They turned to see Fraser standing on the top of the hill. "I'm right glad to see ye safe, Lady Darcy. Laird Robert sent me to find ye. The rest of de Clare's men have surrendered." His gaze fell on the body of John de Clare lying in the sand. "What should we do with him?"

"He'll be taken back to Dunbreggan and given the proper rights. The Murrays will be given back the body of their laird for proper burial."

Fraser nodded. Quinn curled his fingers through Darcy's.

"I'm relieved ye made that choice, love. To stay I mean. It must be mighty strange for ye living in my time and I know ye must be homesick. "

Darcy bit her lip. "Sure there'll be some things I'll miss. My friends, mostly, and I'll always regret not being able to say goodbye. But if there's one thing I've learned in my life it's that chances at happiness are rare. You have to seize them when you get the chance. So, yes, I made the right choice."

"I'm right glad to hear ye say that. It's time we started our journey home then, love."

Darcy cocked her head. "Home. I like the sound of that."

"Me too. And the sooner we get home the sooner Rebecca can get her claws into ye." He winked at her mischievously. "After all, don't we have a wedding to prepare?"

"Are ye ready, lass?" Robert asked.

The laird of the MacFarlane clan was done up in all his finery and Darcy had to admit he scrubbed up rather well. He was standing by the door, ready to escort her downstairs. Darcy's stomach flipped over. Even though she'd dreamed about this moment for the last week, she still felt sick with nerves.

"You look like you've eaten something you shouldn't!" Lily teased.

Lily wore a fine silk gown and carried a bouquet of freshly gathered flowers. She'd agreed to be Darcy's maid of honor - a role that would be reversed when Lily's own wedding came around. It wouldn't be for a little while yet as Lily wanted to wait for her family to make the long trip up from London.

Darcy smiled weakly at her friend's joke. She pulled in a deep breath, straightened her shoulders. "Right. Let's do this."

"Yer getting married lass, not going into battle!" Robert laughed.

He offered her his arm and she took it. They swept out of Robert's solar, Lily walking behind with Darcy's train.

The walk to the great hall seemed to last forever. Surely it didn't normally take this long? Her stomach churned. Her heart hammered in her chest. But not from fear. From excitement.

Today was the day. The day she'd marry the man she loved. The day they'd be joined together forever. She couldn't wait.

Finally they reached the steps down into the great hall and Robert escorted her down, seeming every inch the proud brother-to-be. As soon as Darcy's foot hit the last step the waiting crowd turned to look at her. The great hall was filled with people and the doors had been thrown open and still more people crowded the bailey outside. Everyone wore their best clothing and MacFarlane plaid was in evidence everywhere. After all, they were welcoming a new member into their clan.

Darcy's eyes roved over the crowd, looking for one face. There. Quinn stood by the altar with Fraser and Rebecca. His eyes lit up as he spied Darcy and her heart soared in response. He was so beautiful. And he was hers.

As she moved to stand beside him he filled her vision. The rest of the clan seemed to disappear and there was only him. He grinned at her and his eyes shone. He held out his hand and she took it, allowing Robert to wind the MacFarlane plaid around both their hands, binding them together.

Father Michael, the local priest, stepped forward and began the ceremony. It passed in a blur. All she could think of was Quinn's hand over hers, his eyes fixed on her face.

Then it was over and Quinn was kissing her. Kissing her so deeply it curled her toes and sent the watching clan into a chorus of whoops and cheers.

Quinn pressed his forehead against hers and looked into her eyes. "Hello, wife," he breathed.

Darcy grinned. "Hello, husband."

Robert threw a hand around both their shoulders. "Come on now, both of ye. They'll be plenty of time for mooning over each other later. Don't ye know ye belong to the clan for today? Come on, we're going to have the biggest feast this clan has seen in many a year!"

Laughing, Darcy allowed Robert to lead her and Quinn down the steps into the bailey where an enormous pavilion had been set up. There would be feasting and drinking and dancing and games until the small hours and the whole village had been invited.

Darcy held tight to Quinn as they took pride of place at the head table, Robert and Rebecca seated to either side. All around the pavilion large trestle tables had been arranged and out in the bailey straw bales had been placed for the others.

As a quartet of musicians sprang up, Darcy sat back, taking it all in. Her new family and friends surrounded her. Her new husband sat by her side. She could hardly believe it was real.

"Are ye all right, love?" Quinn asked.

Darcy nodded. "Oh yes. I'm more all right than I've ever been."

Quinn grinned at her. "Me too, love. Look, they're bringing the first course round. We'll be expected to eat before the rest of the clan get served."

Darcy patted her stomach. "I'm not sure I can eat anything. I've been so nervous all morning!"

"None of that, love. Ye have to keep yer strength up - for all the day's festivities but especially for what I have planned for ye when I get ye back to our chamber."

That mischievous grin was on his face again - the one she loved so much. She found herself grinning in response.

"Well, when you put it like that I'm sure I could manage something."

As Quinn had predicted, the celebrations went on late into the night. Darcy had the time of her life. It seemed everyone in the village wanted a word or a dance or to give her their congratulations. Darcy had never felt so valued or so at home.

They were sitting at a table, finally getting some time alone when Quinn leaned over and whispered, "I reckon we could sneak out now, love. What do ye say?"

A little thrill of anticipation went through Darcy. "Let's do it."

They'd almost made it to the stairs when a cheer went up behind them. Darcy turned to see the remaining guests whooping and clapping. Her face flushed red.

Quinn though, merely grinned. "I thank ye for yer encouragement, ye scoundrels! Now if ye'll excuse me, I have a bride to take care of."

He bent and swept a startled Darcy into his arms. The sounds of good-natured suggestions and banter followed them up the stairs.

Quinn kicked open the door to their chamber and then nudged it closed behind them. Robert had given them a magnificent suite right at the top of the castle. It had its own sitting room and a large balcony that gave a stunning view of the vista beyond. The place already felt more like home than Darcy's apartment ever had.

Quinn carried her through the sitting room and into the bedroom. He laid her down carefully on the bed and stood for a minute, looking her over.

She raised herself onto her elbows. "What are you thinking?"

"I'm thinking of how lucky I am," he replied. "Of how beautiful my wife is."

"Well stop thinking and come here," she chuckled.

He obliged, climbing onto the bed and straddling her, his hands to either side of her face. He looked into her eyes for a moment and then leaned down to kiss her. His lips were warm and soft as they gently brushed hers.

"Are ye sure ye wouldnae rather just go to sleep?" he teased. "It's been a long day."

"It has," Darcy agreed. "And it's only going to get longer."

She reached up and tangled her fingers through his hair, pulling him down for a kiss. Quinn obliged. His mouth caressed hers hungrily and his strong hands found the laces of her dress and pulled them free, his hand slipping inside her bodice to cup one of her breasts.

She moaned as he began to caress her, one thumb rubbing her nipple, the other tracing a line of fire down her side.

She grabbed the brooch that held his plaid at his shoulder and unclasped it. Quinn ducked his head, allowing her to deposit the material on the floor. Darcy's eyes roved over his bare torso, watching how the candlelight caught the contours of his muscles. She ran her fingertips over his skin.

Mine, she thought as she looked at him. *This beautiful, amazing man is mine.*

"Here, love," Quinn said. "Ye must be hot in that dress. How about I relieve ye of it?"

He roughly began untying the rest of the laces in her dress. In only moments he was pulling it free, exposing her skin to the cool night air.

Quinn gasped lightly as he looked at her and his manhood bulged between his legs, eager and ready. Darcy ran her fingertips along his length and his eyes slid closed, a deep moan escaping him. She stroked him gently, bringing him to utter arousal until, with a growl, he grabbed her hands and pinned them to the bed by her head.

He was in control. She was at his mercy. She loved it. She lay compliant as he gazed down at her, his breathing already heavy. He nudged her knees apart, the tip of his manhood brushing against her sensitive spot. She tilted her hips, rising up to meet him, inviting him inside, but he didn't give her what she wanted. Not yet.

He teased her, gently caressing her until she moaned with pleasure and need.

"Quinn," Darcy gasped, unable to form any other words. "Oh my god, Quinn."

Sensing her desperate need, Quinn dropped his hips and with one strong thrust, penetrated her, deep and hard. Darcy cried out in bliss, bucking against him. He began to move inside her, driving into her with hard, deep movements. Darcy tilted her hips to meet his thrusts, taking him deep into her core each time.

Fire raced along her nerves. Liquid ecstasy made her skin tingle. She moved in time with Quinn, their breathing becoming ragged, gasps of pleasure filling the air.

The inferno inside Darcy grew and grew, it burned along every sinew in her body until finally it consumed her, and she cried Quinn's name as her climax took her. A second later Quinn jerked as he too, reached his peak.

Quinn looked down at her, his eyes dark with lust. "I love ye, Darcy MacFarlane, do ye know that?"

"Aye, Quinn MacFarlane," she whispered back. "And I love you too."

Quinn rolled onto his back, pulling her into the crook of his arm. After a moment she propped herself on an elbow and tangled the fingers of one hand in his hair.

"There's no time for resting. What were you saying about keeping your strength up? When I'm finished with you you'll need it."

He laughed, then wrapped his arms around her and kissed her. Yes, it was going to be a long, long night.

Choices, lass, a voice whispered. It sounded like the wind whispering in branches. *Did ye make the right one, Darcy Greenway? Come, so I may speak with ye.*

Darcy woke with a start. It was dark, sometime in the deep night and moonlight was streaming through the window, illuminating the rug-covered floor. By her side Quinn snored softly, one arm wrapped protectively around her.

Careful not to wake him, Darcy extricated herself from his embrace and climbed out of bed. She pulled on a robe and padded across the floor to the balcony. Opening the door, she stepped out.

The moon hung low in the sky and the Highlands stretching out before her looked like they'd been dusted with icing sugar. Darcy sucked in a deep breath, savoring the clean air in her lungs. Around her, Dunbreggan slept.

"Well? Do ye ken the answer to my question, dearie?"

Darcy spun to find Irene MacAskill standing on the balcony beside her. The small woman stood in the shadows, only her eyes gleaming in the moonlight. Darcy had learned not to be surprised by anything this woman might do although it was still unsettling the way she appeared from nowhere.

"I heard your voice in my dream," she replied. "But I didn't expect to see you again. You said your work here was done."

"Almost but not quite. My kind are bound by rules and I must obey them. Anyone given the choice must also be given a chance to change their mind." Her gaze sharpened. "One chance and one chance only. So I ask again: are ye sure ye made the right choice? Or will you run away once more, Darcy Greenway?"

Darcy glanced through the door to where Quinn was sleeping. He'd turned over and now had one arm and one leg dangling over the side of the bed. She smiled fondly.

"I'm done running," she replied. "I think all my life I've been running, searching for him. Now I've found him. So yes, of course I made the right choice."

Irene MacAskill's eyes twinkled. "Quinn said exactly the same thing."

Darcy's eyebrows rose. "You've already spoken to him?"

"Aye. Didnae I say everyone is given one chance?"

Darcy paused. "And what would happen if one of us had changed our minds?"

Irene shrugged. "Ye'd have gone back to yer lives having no memory that any of this had happened."

Darcy wasn't sure what to make of that. She shifted uncomfortably. "I need to ask you something. A favor."

Irene MacAskill studied Darcy with a sharp gaze. "Asking favors of the fae can be a dangerous game, lass. Ye never know when that favor might be called in. Did ye know that?"

Darcy nodded. "So I've been told. But it's important to me, Irene. Please?"

"What would ye ask?"

"I know you can travel through time. Could you go to my friend, Gretchen? Tell her I'm okay?"

"Gretchen Matthews? Mayhap she has her own part to play in this story, yet."

"What does that mean?"

The old woman just shook her head. "That's not for ye to ken. Very well. As you're my favorite veterinarian I'll do if for ye."

"I'm the *only* veterinarian," Darcy said dryly.

"Aye, that as well."

"Darcy?" Quinn's voice called from the bedroom. "What are ye doing on the balcony?"

"Looks like yer new husband is getting cold. Ye'd better go. I'll do what I promised."

Darcy was suddenly overcome with affection for this strange old woman. She leaned forward and wrapped her in a hug. "Thank you, Irene. Thank you for everything."

Irene returned the hug then stepped back, smiling. "Go on lass, yer future is waiting for ye."

Darcy glanced at the doorway. When she glanced back, Irene MacAskill was gone. "Goodbye," Darcy whispered. "Until we meet again."

Then she walked through the door to where her future waited.

Also by Katy Baker

Broken Fire
Chasing Fire (A Steamy New Adult Romance)
Kissing Fire (A Steamy New Adult Romance)
Embracing Fire (A Steamy New Adult Romance)
Broken Fire (The Complete Collection)

Don't Touch
Touchpaper
Powderkeg
Firework

Falling for the bad boy
Gripped
Torn

Immortals of London
The Book of Prime
The Rise of the One
The Rogue Hunter
The Shadow of the Moon
The Lost One
The Broken Shard

My Best Friend's Father
At The Party
At The Apartment
At The Office
My Best Friend's Father (The Complete Collection)

Reach For Me

This Beautiful Moment
This Beautiful Betrayal
This Beautiful Forever
This Beautiful Everything (Reach For Me Complete Series)

The Boy Next Door
Exploring The Boy Next Door
Teasing The Boy Next Door
Loving The Boy Next Door
The Boy Next Door - The Complete Collection

Standalone
Immortals of London (The Complete Series)
Don't Touch (The Complete New Adult Romance series)
Dreams of a Highlander

20567444R00120

Made in the USA
San Bernardino, CA
28 December 2018